WICKED WHIMSY

An Ivy Morgan Mystery Book 11

LILY HARPER HART

HarperHart Publications

Copyright © 2018 by Lily Harper Hart

All rights reserved.

No part of this book may be reproduced in any form or by any electronic or mechanical means, including information storage and retrieval systems, without written permission from the author, except for the use of brief quotations in a book review.

❦ Created with Vellum

One

"What are you doing again?"

Jack Harker stood next to his truck, a travel mug of coffee clutched in his hand, and stared at his fiancée Ivy Morgan with a look of confusion and resignation. He wasn't exactly a morning person – neither was Ivy, for that matter – but the fact that she was up at the crack of dawn and appeared to be preparing to spend the entire day in the woods was enough to throw him for a loop.

For her part, Ivy could do nothing but roll her eyes. She was used to Jack's exaggerated grumpiness in the morning. She not only accepted it but often reveled in it because, to her, it proved how well suited they were for one another. She liked to be grumpy before ten, too. Mornings weren't meant to be enjoyed, after all. There was one lone exception to that rule.

"I'm spending the day morel hunting with Max," Ivy replied without hesitation. "I told you this last night."

The only thing Jack could remember about the previous evening was that Ivy chose to serve him dinner in bed ... while naked. Everything other than that flew out the window as they enjoyed each other's company, and a blessedly quiet house.

"Fine. You're going morel hunting." Jack used his free hand to play with a strand of Ivy's pink-streaked hair. When he first met her a year before – almost exactly a year before actually – he found her hair weird and yet beguiling. Now he found everything about the woman he loved more than life itself beguiling. The hair was simply part of her. "Why do you feel the need to tell me this, though? You've been morel hunting every day for the past week."

"Well, I thought we were getting married," Ivy started, causing Jack to furrow his brow.

"We *are* getting married," Jack interjected. "Don't even try to get out of it."

"I don't want to get out of it." Ivy's smile was whimsical. "Although, speaking of that, we should probably pick a date so I can get my mother and aunt off my back. They're convinced we have a lot of planning to do and can't even start until we pick a date."

"Fine. Let's get married tomorrow."

Ivy's grin turned wicked. "You just want an immediate honeymoon."

"I'm fine pretending we're on a honeymoon," Jack countered. "I simply can't wait to call you 'my wife' and point out to everyone I meet that I snagged the prettiest woman in all the land."

Despite herself, Ivy was a little charmed. "You're smooth."

"I do my best." Jack pressed a tiny kiss to the tip of her nose. "As for setting a date, I don't care. Pick what you want. Sooner works better for me, but it's up to you."

Ivy narrowed her sea-blue eyes. "I don't think it's supposed to work that way."

"I'm easy."

"I already know that." Ivy poked his side and did a little hip-wiggling dance to let him know she was teasing. "I think we should sit down and pick a day. I ... please?"

Jack couldn't deny her so he simply nodded. "Tonight. We'll do it over dinner. How does that sound?"

Ivy was secretly relieved he gave in so easily. She wasn't keen on picking a date without backup. She was convinced she would pick the wrong date and then things would officially fall apart and it would all be her fault. She needed support, even if it was only of the emotional variety. "Thank you."

"Yeah, yeah." Jack tapped his cheek to prod Ivy into giving him a kiss in thanks.

Ivy rolled her eyes, although it was only for form's sake, and slid closer so she could do just that. Jack took her by surprise when he left his travel mug on the hood of his truck and wrapped both of his arms around her slim waist, smacking a loud and playful kiss against her mouth as he dipped her low.

"You're being a goofball," Ivy laughed, giggling harder as he moved his lips to her neck and made obnoxious chewing noises. "I think you might be the king of goofballs."

"Only around you." Jack gave her another kiss before righting her. His eyes were filled with mirth but there was a serious edge to his expression when he looked her up and down. "Now tell me what you're doing with the rest of your day again. I'm not sure I was listening when you started."

Ivy heaved out a sigh. "I'm going morel hunting with Max. I told you already, but I wanted to remind you in case you come back for lunch and I'm not here. I know how you worry."

"That's what happens when you love someone." Jack pursed his lips as he ran the scenario through his head. While Max Morgan wasn't always the most mature man in the room, as Ivy's brother, Jack knew he would sacrifice his life to keep his sister safe. That was Max's best trait in Jack's book. "How long are you guys planning on hanging out in the woods?"

"We're making a day of it."

Jack ran a hand through his dark hair as he regarded her. "What about your nursery?"

Ivy's main way of supporting herself was a well-regarded plant nursery located just through the woods on the other side of the property where they stood. Winter was her dead time in the business, but spring was a busy time and she'd been spending hours doing laborious work in her greenhouse to prepare.

"I got ahead," Ivy replied. "I've been planning for this day for weeks."

Jack knew better than to make a big deal out of Ivy's need to hunt for mushrooms that he, unfortunately, believed tasted like gritty wet sponges. She loved the stupid things and they were only available in northern Lower Michigan for a limited time each year. Still, since she often found trouble when traipsing through the woods, he couldn't allow her to leave without issuing a warning.

"Fine." He gave her an adoring smile. "Have fun mushroom hunting with your brother."

"I wasn't asking your permission." Ivy was matter of fact as she squared her shoulders. "I was simply telling you where I would be."

"I should have seen that coming." Jack chuckled dryly as he shook his head. "Please try to be back before dark. I will definitely worry if you're still out there after dark."

"I'll be back before dark." Ivy rolled to the balls of her feet and pressed a kiss to the corner of Jack's mouth. "I'm going to make cream of morel soup for dinner tonight."

Jack managed to keep his expression neutral, but just barely. "That sounds ... great."

Ivy stared at him for a long beat. She wanted to drag out his torture for as long as she could manage, but he was so earnest sometimes, so determined to please her, that she couldn't bring herself to be mean. "I'm making two batches of the soup. A big one for me to freeze so I can have morel soup all year and a smaller batch with regular mushrooms for you."

"And that's why I love you." Jack gave her another kiss and grinned. "By the way ... I love you more than anything." His voice was barely a whisper against the ridge of her ear, causing the hair on the back of her neck to stand on end. "I'll romance your socks off later."

"That sounds like a plan." Ivy pulled back and watched him open the truck door. "You be good today. Safe."

Jack was a police officer, although Shadow Lake wasn't exactly known as a hotbed of crime. Still, Ivy occasionally worried about him. That was nothing compared to the worry Jack felt when Ivy found trouble.

"You're the one who needs to stay safe," Jack countered. "If you could refrain from finding trouble in the woods today, that would be great."

Ivy snorted, genuinely amused. "I promise."

"That's all I ask."

"I SAY WE MAKE a competition out of it."

An hour later, Max Morgan led the way into the woods. He clutched an old pillowcase in his hand and added a bit of spring to his step as he studied the ground.

"You want to make a competition out of what?" Ivy asked, following her brother's lead and staring at the base of a nearby tree.

"Morel hunting," Max replied. "Whoever finds the most mushrooms should win something."

Ivy pulled up short and slowly shifted her gaze to her brother's face. "What do you think you should win?"

"I'm thinking you should make me a chocolate cake." Max's grin was mischievous. "That one you know I like ... with the sprinkles."

Ivy made a dismissive sound in the back of her throat. "And why would I want to do that? I'm already making cream of morel soup to freeze for the entire family. That should be gift enough."

"I want cake, too."

"And what about if I win?" Ivy challenged. "What are you going to do for me if I win?"

"You won't win."

Ivy blinked hard. "Excuse me?" She was used to her brother's out-of-control ego, but she wasn't expecting this. "I'm just as good at finding morels as you are. In fact, I'm better."

"You're cute." Max beamed at her, the look of an older brother who adored his younger sibling. "You're also dreaming."

Ivy scowled. She was competitive by nature and she couldn't help it that Max's words juiced up her need to succeed. "Oh, it's on."

Max smirked at his sister's back as she focused her attention on a group of trees and sprinted in that direction. He loved Ivy's competitive spirit. He fostered it in her when she was younger because he often worried she spent too much time trapped in her head. The fact that he enjoyed competing with her as much as she enjoyed competing with him was merely a side benefit. "It's definitely on."

The duo fell into an amiable silence as they spent the next few minutes collecting mushrooms. They didn't need to talk to spend time together. Still, Ivy was more comfortable with the silence than Max and eventually he felt the need to fill in the gaps.

"Have you heard from Harper?"

The question caught Ivy off guard. Harper Harlow, ghost hunter extraordinaire and one of the only females Ivy had ever felt truly bonded with, lived in southeastern Michigan. She visited Shadow Lake almost a week before – only leaving five days ago – and helped solve a rather intriguing mystery with Ivy at her side.

Since Ivy was quickly coming to the realization that she might just be a witch – she wasn't happy with the label, but it seemed to be the one that best fit the things she could do – she and Harper bonded from practically the moment they met. Harper could see and talk to ghosts. Ivy had a special psychic streak and had talked to a few ghosts throughout the years, too. The two women were both snarky and strong. Harper's best friend Zander teased they were like two peas in a pod, although that's exactly how Ivy felt. From the moment she met the gregarious blonde, something simply clicked between them.

"She called yesterday," Ivy replied as she used a stick to poke at some fallen leaves. "She says they're working on a case that is giving her a headache – and that Zander always gives her a headache, so things are doubly bad – but everything else is good."

Max paused long enough to give his sister a searching look. "How many times have you talked to her since she left?"

Ivy recognized the tone and balked. "What does that matter?"

"How many times?" Max pressed.

"Once or twice." Ivy was purposely evasive as she leaned over to pluck a small group of morels from the ground. "It's not a big deal. I wish you guys would stop treating it like a big deal."

"It *is* a big deal," Max countered, refusing to back down. "You don't usually like women. In fact, you hate most of the ones you've come into contact with."

"That's usually because they hate me first," Ivy pointed out. "I don't hate people for no reason."

"That's very true." Max adopted a reasonable tone. "You wait until you're hated before hating back. That's very mature of you."

"Ugh. I hate it when you do this." Ivy moved to another tree. "You're trying to get me going, knock me off my game so you'll win the competition. It's not going to work. I won't allow it to work."

Max feigned innocence. "Hey! I'm merely showing interest in my baby sister because I love her. I'm a good big brother."

Ivy didn't buy that for a moment. "You're trying to throw me off my game."

Max chuckled. "I'm not. I was honestly curious. I haven't seen you in the past few days. I knew you were a little sad when Harper left so I wanted to make sure you were okay."

Ivy turned defensive. "Sad? Who said I was said?"

Max saw no reason to lie. "Jack."

"Jack said I was sad?"

"He might've mentioned that you seemed a little down," Max clarified, recognizing his sister's tone and quickly moving to repair what damage he could. "Don't get all worked up about that, by the way. Jack is a good guy and he cares about you. He simply mentioned it to me when we talked."

"And when was that?"

"About ten minutes before I arrived at your house."

Ivy did the math in her head. "That was after he said goodbye to me," she mused, anger and amusement warring for supremacy in her busy mind. "I wonder why he called you. Did he really sound worried?"

"No. The Harper stuff was just a side conversation. He wanted to talk to me about something else."

Ivy was officially intrigued. "And what was the something else?"

If Max sensed a trap, he didn't show it. Instead he happily walked through the open door and took the obvious bait. "He wanted me to make sure that you didn't wander off and get into trouble. He says he doesn't want to spend the day worrying about you if he doesn't have to."

Ivy wasn't sure what to make of the statement. "Why does he naturally assume I'll find trouble?"

Max snickered at his sister's annoyed expression. "Oh, I wonder. Perhaps it's because in the year since he's met you he's had to save you no less than ten times."

"That's a vicious lie." Ivy's anger flared to life. "First off, I don't ever need to be saved. I can save myself."

"Yes, you're a self-rescuing princess," Max drawled. "You always have been."

"Secondly, I've saved him as many times as he has saved me," Ivy continued, as if her brother hadn't said a word. "He's barely had to save me at all. It only happened once in fact ... er, maybe twice."

Max cocked a challenging eyebrow and remained silent.

"Three times at the most," Ivy persisted. "He's totally exaggerating."

"That's neither here nor there," Max said after a beat, licking his lips. "He merely wanted to make sure that I kept an eye on you. He doesn't want you finding trouble."

"I never find trouble." Ivy was annoyed but that didn't stop her from keeping her head in the game. "Ha!" She darted toward a large tree, which had a regular cornucopia of morels poking out from beneath a bunch of leaves around the base. "Mine! I claim all of these as mine."

Max scowled when he caught sight of the rich haul. "I should spend more time looking for mushrooms and less looking out for you."

"I agree," Ivy concurred, bobbing her head as she happily shoved mushrooms in her pillowcase. "You should definitely focus on the mushrooms. I'm going to kick the crap out of you otherwise. In fact ... ." She trailed off when the hair on the back of her neck stood on end.

Her gaze was slow as she let it bounce around the immediate area, her back going stiff. She didn't see anything out of the ordinary and yet she felt as if something big was about to happen. Whatever that something was, Ivy instinctively knew Jack wouldn't like it.

"Max."

For his part, Max was focused on the ground rather than his sister. "If you think I'm going to let you win, you have another think coming.

I won't let you distract me any more than you'll let me distract you. This is a competition, after all. May the best Morgan win."

Ivy licked her lips as her heart rate increased. She could sense trouble coming, although she had no idea from which direction.

"Max."

"Don't try to distract me." Max haphazardly waved his hand without looking at Ivy's face. "It's not going to work. Nothing is going to distract me from beating the pants off you."

As if on cue, the bushes to the left of them exploded as a boy ran through them, tripping over his own feet as he fell hard against the ground. Tears coursed down his cheeks, his clothing was snarled and ripped in several places, and he looked as if the world was about to end.

"They shot him!" he bellowed, his eyes going wide when he saw Ivy. "They shot him and he needs help! They're coming. We have to get out of here."

Two

For several moments, Ivy felt as if she was caught in quicksand. Her mind worked at a fantastic rate, but she was paralyzed with fear and inaction as she tried to decide what to do. Thankfully for her, Max was the first to step forward and take control of the situation.

"Slow down." He moved to the spot in front of the boy and forced a friendly smile onto his face. "Tell us exactly what happened so we can figure out the best way to help you."

The boy, whom Ivy figured to be in his early teens, looked frustrated more than anything else as his gaze bounced between them. "Did you not hear what I said? My father has been shot! There's someone in these woods who wants to hurt me. We have to get out of here."

"I *did* hear you." Max purposely maintained an air of calmness as he leaned over to stare into the boy's eyes. "We need more information if we're going to be able to help, though. Let's start with your name."

The boy's eyes, green and wild, widened as he looked over his shoulder. Ivy followed his gaze, half-expecting a masked marauder to step through the trees and attack. The woods, however, remained quiet.

"What does my name matter?"

"We need to know," Max pressed, lightly resting his hand on the young man's shoulder. "Please. Tell us your name and we'll go from there."

"Josh." He swallowed hard. "My name is Josh."

"Good." Max adopted his most soothing tone. "Josh what?"

"Josh Masters."

"Okay, Josh." Max gripped his pillowcase and straightened. "I want you to walk us back through the woods to where you last saw your father and tell us what happened on the way. Do you think you can do that?"

Josh, clearly frustrated with Max's reaction, turned a set of pleading emerald eyes on Ivy. "We have to run."

For her part, Ivy was uncertain how to respond. "Max, maybe we should take him back to the house and call Jack and Brian."

"Or maybe you should call Jack right now before we lose a signal and tell him we're heading into the woods," Max countered. "Tell him to head out and we'll provide more details as soon as we can."

Ivy involuntarily cringed at the suggestion. The last thing Jack said to her was that he wanted her to have a good time but stay out of trouble. He was so adamant he actually called Max to reiterate how he wanted the day to go. He most certainly wasn't going to like the turn of events. "He's going to be mad."

"Yeah, he is," Max agreed. "It's not as if we can control it, though. We're doing the best we can." He kept his smile in place for Josh's benefit, even though it looked a bit deranged given the circumstances. "Call him anyway. If Josh's father is out here, he's probably in need of medical attention."

Ivy nodded as she dug in her pocket for her phone. "Okay. I hope this is some sort of elaborate hoax, though."

Max stared hard into Josh's eyes. "That would be nice, but I doubt very much that's how things will turn out."

MAX WAS RIGHT ABOUT things turning out differently. After a lot of hemming and hawing – and one bout of foot stomping and bellowing – Josh managed to pick his way back through the woods and lead Ivy and Max to the spot where he last saw his father.

Abraham Masters, the boy's father, was dead on the ground. His sightless eyes were pointed at the sky and a pillowcase sat abandoned on the uneven wood carpet next to what looked to be a small orange bag. There was an ugly wound in his chest, blood completely covering his shirt and coat. It was obvious that emergency personnel wouldn't be able to save him.

"I'll call Jack again," Ivy said, resigned. "Brian should be able to find us in here. We're not far from the road."

"I'll stick with Josh." Max slid his arm around the boy's shoulders. For some reason – and Ivy was certain it had to do with shock – Josh couldn't tear his eyes away from his father. The tableau was horrible and not something a young boy should see, but he couldn't look away.

"I'll head out to the road and flag them down," Ivy offered. "I won't be gone long."

Max mutely nodded as he focused on Josh. "It's going to be okay, Josh. We're going to get you out of here really soon. We'll figure this out."

Ivy gave them one more look before breaking into a slow jog and pointing herself toward the trees on her right. She waited until she was almost through the foliage before calling Jack a second time and turning her expectant eyes to the country road.

It didn't take Jack and his partner long to track her down. Jack was out of the cruiser like a shot before Brian Nixon even had the vehicle in park.

"Are you okay?" Jack pulled her flush against his chest, smoothing her hair in the same manner he tried to smooth his own frazzled nerves. He knew she was safe because of the first call, but the idea of her running around the woods when a shooter might be on the loose was traumatizing.

"I'm fine." Ivy awkwardly patted his back. "He came out of nowhere, though. One minute Max and I were arguing about who was going to win the contest and the next ... well ... we had a terrified boy to contend with."

"Did you find his father?" Brian asked as he joined them.

Ivy nodded. "He's dead."

"Are you sure?"

"Yeah. There's no doubt about that. He's been shot."

"How far away was he from you and Max?" Jack asked. "I mean ... was he close enough that you guys could've been hurt if you ran into whoever did that?"

Ivy tilted her head to the side, considering. She honestly hadn't even thought about the possibility. "We didn't hear a gunshot. Perhaps it happened when we were still inside. He was about three-quarters of a mile from us, so we probably should've heard something but ... we didn't."

"How long were you in the woods before he found you?" Brian asked.

"Not long. We were barely clear of the house."

"You were probably inside then." Brian started typing on his phone. "How far in are they?"

"About a quarter of a mile. Max is with Josh."

Jack cocked an eyebrow. "Josh?"

"Josh Masters," Ivy supplied. "His father is Abraham Masters. I didn't recognize the name – or face – but I didn't look too closely."

"Of course not, honey." Jack pressed a kiss to her forehead before releasing her. "You don't have to stay if you don't want to. Just direct us to the spot and head back to the house. It's okay."

Ivy opened her mouth to argue with the sentiment, but Brian did it before she could.

"It's not okay," Brian countered, shaking his head. "She has to stay out here and answer some questions. She doesn't get special treatment simply because she's engaged to one of the detectives on the case."

Jack scowled. "I wasn't suggesting she get special treatment."

"That's exactly what you were doing."

Jack looked to Ivy for support and found her lips curving. "I wasn't giving you special treatment."

"I like getting special treatment," Ivy volunteered as she patted his arm. "I can't leave, though. I feel responsible. I need to stay until we get Josh home. He's ... upset."

"I can understand that." Brian gestured toward the woods, prodding Ivy to turn on her heel and lead the way back to the scene. "Has he said anything to you that would indicate what he was doing out here, or what happened?"

"When he first showed up he said his father was shot and that *they* were coming," Ivy replied. "He didn't say who he was and we didn't press him too much. Max kind of took control because I wasn't sure what to do. I think we both thought there was a chance Josh was playing a game or got confused. It turns out that wasn't the case."

"Yeah."

Jack linked his fingers with Ivy's as they walked, taking a moment to enjoy the tactile contact. He would have to turn to business as soon as they reached the body but, for now, he had a few minutes to thank his lucky stars that she was all right ... again. "Did he say anything else?"

"He was reluctant to go back into the woods with us when Max asked him to take us to his father," Ivy explained. "I think that was fear. He ran when his father was shot. His survival instincts took over. Going back forced him to see what he left behind."

"He did the right thing," Jack countered. "If he'd stayed, in all likelihood he would've been killed, too."

"Oh, I know that," Ivy reassured him. "I just don't think he realizes it yet. I feel sorry for him."

"We all feel sorry for him," Brian supplied. "We have to find out who did this, though. That's the most important thing. It's too late to go back in time and save Abraham Masters. It's not, however, too late to get him justice. That's what we're going to do."

TO IVY'S UTTER SURPRISE, Josh eagerly pulled away from Max upon her return and threw his arms around her waist. Since she'd barely talked to the boy – certainly hadn't bonded with him – she was dumbfounded by his greeting.

"Are you okay?"

Josh nodded but kept his face buried in her shoulder. "I didn't know if you were going to come back."

"Of course I came back." Ivy stroked the back of his soft hair as she met Max's quizzical gaze. She read her brother's shrug as him saying he had no idea what was going on either. "I just had to make sure the police knew where to enter and how to find us."

"The police?" Josh reluctantly pulled back his face so he could study Brian and Jack with something akin to hostility. "Are you sure they're the police?"

"I'm sure."

"They could be the people who did this," Josh argued. "I only saw one person shoot my father but ... it might have been more. I was too afraid to look around for another person, but it could've been them."

Josh was clearly paranoid – and Ivy couldn't blame him – but his reaction to Jack and Brian threw her for a loop.

"I swear they're the police." Ivy kept her voice calm. "I've known Brian – er, Detective Nixon – since I was a little girl. He's been friends with my family for years. As for Detective Harker over there, he might look tall and mean, but he's actually a big pussycat."

Jack scowled. "Thanks for that, honey." He held his hands up in a placating manner as he slowly approached Josh. He didn't want to startle the boy. It was clear he'd been through something traumatic. "The rest of what Ms. Morgan said is true. I am a police officer. I'm here to help you and your father."

"He's dead." Josh was emotionless. "You can't help him."

"We can get justice for him," Brian clarified. "We can help you, though. We need some information to do that."

"I don't have any information," Josh shot back. "I don't know who did this. For all I know, you did this."

He wasn't about to let go of his suspicions. Ivy understood that, although the boy's determination to be belligerent taxed her patience. "Josh, look at me." When he didn't immediately acquiesce, Ivy adopted her best "I'm the boss and you have to listen to me" voice. "Look at me," she repeated.

Josh slowly turned so he was facing her, his arms still wrapped tightly around her waist as if he was using her as a life preserver. "What?"

"Jack and Brian want to help. If you want them to find the person who did this, you need to tell them exactly what you remember. They need a place to start looking."

"I ... ." Josh heaved out a sigh and nodded, slowly releasing his iron grip on Ivy as he stared at the two police officers. "What do you need me to do?"

"We need you to start at the beginning," Brian prodded gently, his eyes sweeping over Abraham Masters' prone body as he scanned the area. "For starters, what were you guys doing out here? Are you local?"

"We live in Bellaire," Josh volunteered, his voice low but strong. "We come over to Shadow Lake every few months or so, but not very often. We came today because my father has been teaching me how to shoot a gun. He thought we could do some target practice and hunt for morels at the same time. He loves morels."

Ivy's eyes briefly flicked to the pillowcase on the ground. It looked half full. They'd obviously been in the woods a decent amount of time before it happened. "I love morels, too," she offered. "That's what Max and I were doing out here."

"You came from Bellaire," Brian noted as he jotted down information in the small notebook he carried. "Do you remember where your father parked when you arrived?"

"I ... um ... ." Josh screwed up his face in concentration. "I'm honestly not sure," he replied finally. "I don't spend a lot of time paying attention to the roads. My father seemed to know where he was going."

"Did you see any landmarks?" Jack asked. "Like ... was there a road sign close by? Or perhaps it was a paved road rather than a dirt one."

"It was definitely a paved road," Josh provided. "Also, um, I'm pretty sure there was a greenhouse close by. I saw the sun hitting the windows. There might even have been more than one."

Jack exchanged a quick look with Ivy. "That means they must have parked close to your nursery. That will definitely cut down the search area."

"Tell us what happened when you hit the woods," Brian instructed. "Your dad had a pillowcase for the mushrooms, right? You said you were going to practice shooting. Where is the gun he brought?"

"I ... don't know." Josh's eyes widened as he looked around the clearing. "He had it in one of those things you carry on your back. It was like a bag shaped like a gun, with straps and stuff."

"I know what you're talking about." Brian bobbed his head. "Was he carrying that across his back?"

"Yeah, but he had it around his arm at the time that it happened."

"Was the gun loaded?" Jack asked.

"No." Josh was solemn as he shook his head. "You're never supposed to carry a loaded gun. My father has been teaching me proper gun safety. He said if I learned everything the right way he would buy me a gun of my own before hunting season this year."

"It's good he was teaching you the right way to handle a firearm," Brian acknowledged. "Tell us what happened after that."

"I don't know," Josh hedged. "We were talking about how bad the Pistons were this year and Dad said maybe we could go to a Cleveland game next year because it wasn't that far away. He was carrying the pillowcase because he was better at finding mushrooms than me.

"Then I heard a noise," he continued, swallowing hard. "I heard a branch snap or something. I thought it was Dad and looked at him first. He was white, though. Like ... really white. He was holding up his hands like they do in movies."

"Then what?" Jack prodded.

"It all happened so fast."

"I know." Jack awkwardly patted his hand against Josh's shoulder. "We need you to tell us."

"There was a man standing right there." Josh pointed toward a specific spot about ten feet from where his father's body lay sprawled on the ground. "I don't know where he came from."

"How was he dressed?" Brian asked.

"Green pants. Black boots. A grayish kind of shirt. He had on one of those winter masks, the type you wear when you're snowmobiling to make sure your face doesn't hurt when you're done."

"The knit kind you roll down this way?" Ivy asked for clarification's sake.

Josh nodded. "Yeah. It was black."

"Did he say anything?" Jack asked.

"I ... don't know." Josh wrinkled his forehead as he thought back to the event. "I know this is going to sound weird, but I don't think my ears were working right. They were kind of muffled or something, like I was wearing a hat and had it pulled low. I wasn't wearing a hat, though."

"That's okay." Brian forced a grim smile. "I know what you're talking about. We can come back to that. Did your father say anything?"

"Yeah. He said 'what are you doing?'."

"Did the man answer?"

"I don't think so. I don't really know what happened or how long it took, but the next thing I know my father was yelling for me to run. He was loud and bossy, and I was afraid ... like really afraid. I ran because I didn't know what else to do."

"You did the right thing," Jack said gently. "Your father was right to tell you to run and you did the right thing."

Josh didn't look convinced that was true. "But I ran and he's dead. How can that be the right thing?"

"You can't look at it that way," Ivy countered. "You ran and you're still alive. How can that be wrong?"

"But what if my father would still be alive if I stayed?"

"You can't know that. Odds are you might be dead, too, if you stayed."

"And you can't know that," Josh said. "I shouldn't have left him."

"You'll never be able to know if things would've been different if you stayed," Jack supplied. "You did what you had to do. I'm sure your father would be so happy to know that you're still here, that you managed to escape."

"I hope so." Josh looked lost and forlorn. "I don't feel very happy about it."

Three

Jack sent Ivy and Max back to the cottage with Josh in tow, pulling Ivy aside long enough to suggest she get as much information from Josh about his family as possible before focusing on the scene.

Brian called for a state police tech team and then carefully wandered around the small clearing as they waited for more help to arrive.

"This doesn't make a lot of sense to me," he said after a few minutes of quiet contemplation. "Why would a killer come out here to take out an enemy?"

"We don't know that Abraham was a specific target," Jack pointed out. "It could've been a crime of opportunity."

"But ... why?"

"Who knows why," Jack replied. "Maybe it's another case like Nelson Delgado trying to hunt people in the woods because he's nuts." He scowled at his own mention of Nelson, a man who lost his mind and decided hunting people was more fun than animals. "It could be something like that."

"I guess." Brian clearly wasn't convinced. "What are the odds we would have two nutbags like that in a month? They can't be good."

Something occurred to Jack. "Unless Nelson had a partner. Maybe we didn't completely solve the last one. Maybe Nelson was working with someone and now that person has decided to pick up where they left off."

"I guess that's possible, but it doesn't feel right." Brian straightened his shoulders. "If the killer came through here like Josh said there was no way for Abraham to avoid what happened. Everything is out in the open and there's no place to hide."

"Okay." Jack followed his partner's thought process. "If we're dealing with a hunting rifle, though, the killer probably had more than one shell in the barrel. Why not kill both Abraham and Josh? Why let the boy get away?"

"We don't know that he willingly let that happen."

"No, but Josh was terrified," Jack pointed out. "You heard him. I think he was already going into shock before the first shot was even fired. He probably didn't put a lot of effort into picking a route and hiding his tracks when he ran."

"True." Brian mimed shooting an invisible person. "Bam. I've shot Abraham. This is after he's told his son to run. He obviously recognized they were in real danger, although how he knew that if the killer didn't speak is beyond me."

"Oh, I don't know," Jack countered. "If I was in the woods with my son and a stranger dressed like what Josh described showed up, I would definitely be on the alert. Also, Josh admits he can't be sure if the man said anything. He said his ears weren't working correctly."

"Shock."

Jack bobbed his head. "Definitely shock. For all we know, the killer held an entire conversation with the father. We need to give Josh time to decompress before talking to him again. I'm sure Ivy and Max will help with that."

"I'm sure they will, too." Brian rubbed the back of his neck as he turned in a slow and deliberate circle. "Ivy's house is back that way." He gestured over his shoulder. "She said they were barely clear of the house when Josh stumbled upon them. That means he ran in that direction.

"Since I'm going to guess Josh merely ran and didn't think about anything but getting away, that means he ran past the killer," he continued. "Why would he do that?"

"Panic," Jack answered simply. "He panicked and ran in the direction he was facing."

"So why didn't the killer take advantage of his mental situation and kill him?" Brian challenged. "Why purposely leave a witness like that?"

Jack turned grim. "I see what you're getting at."

"I think we have two possibilities," Brian continued. "I think either the killer purposely let Josh go because he didn't realize the boy would find help so quickly and he wanted to turn it into a game of sorts, perhaps stalk him, or that he simply couldn't bring himself to kill a kid."

"There is a third possibility," Jack noted. "Maybe the killer did know Abraham Masters. Maybe he followed Abraham out here and wanted to kill him for a specific purpose. If the kid didn't fit into that purpose, there was no reason to kill him."

"Except the kid can identify his father's killer."

"No, the kid saw a guy in a mask," Jack corrected. "He was too messed up to identify the killer. Maybe whoever did this understood that. Maybe he recognized Josh was too terrified and wasn't worried about letting him go.

"It's hard enough to kill a grown man," he continued. "It's harder to kill a defenseless boy."

"So, are you suggesting we have a killer with a conscience?"

Jack wasn't sure how to answer and held his hands palms out. "I'm saying we have a puzzle on our hands and we'd better start putting it together if we want to make sense of it."

"Yeah, well, if you have any suggestions on that, I'm all ears."

"Let's see what the tech team finds. They might be able to point us in the right direction."

IVY SETTLED JOSH AT her small kitchen table with Max before setting about to make some hot chocolate. She was something of a health food enthusiast – a vegetarian who enjoyed a good carrot stick as much as a cookie on most occasions – but she had a few items that would appeal to a teenager.

"I have some cookies." Ivy rummaged in the refrigerator until she came back with a plate of chocolate chip cookies. "I just made them yesterday."

"I see you've been holding out on me," Max said, going for jocularity even though the situation didn't seem to warrant it. "Did you hide those earlier because you knew I would eat them all?"

"I hid them so Jack would have something to munch on when he got home tonight," Ivy replied. "I can make more, though. It will just take a second for the water to boil and then we'll add hot chocolate to the mix."

"Yum." Max's eyes sparkled. "You know how much I love hot chocolate."

"I do," Ivy confirmed before turning her full attention on Josh. "How about you, sweetie? Do you like hot chocolate?"

For his part, Josh had become more and more morose as they hiked through the woods. He barely spared Ivy's cottage a glance when they arrived in the yard and she led him to the front porch. Once inside, he sank into one of the chairs she indicated and stared into nothing. The reality of his situation was slowly starting to sink in and Ivy felt helpless in the wake of the boy's grief.

"It's fine," Josh replied woodenly. "Whatever you have is fine."

"Well, it's going to be hot chocolate." Ivy forced a smile as she sat in a chair next to him. "I know you're upset. I can't even imagine what you're going through. You and your father were obviously close."

"He wanted to teach me things." Josh's affect was dull and muted, as if he'd just woken up and needed eight cups of coffee to spur him to movement. "He always said that was important. Like ... he wanted to teach me how to change spark plugs on his truck and stuff like that. He said there were certain things all men should know."

"I think that's very wise," Max intoned. "I wish my father had taught me things like that."

Ivy made a face. Max was not the sort of guy who enjoyed working on a car engine. He liked construction well enough, fiddling around with wood and home projects. Vehicles were another story. He was as helpless as she was when it came to a vehicle. Still, that wasn't the sort of thing Josh needed to hear now.

"That was very smart of your father," Ivy encouraged. "I bet you have a lot of good memories of working with him in the garage."

"Yeah." Josh rubbed the crease between his eyebrows as he stared at the table. "What's going to happen to me now?"

Ivy was expecting the question, although perhaps not worded the way Josh opted to express himself. "Well, we need to talk about that." She slowly returned to the stove and removed the kettle when it began whistling. She had three mugs ready for water and cocoa already sitting on the counter. "Where is your mother, sweetie? Is she close?"

"She's dead." Josh's response was so bland and devoid of emotion it floored Ivy.

"Dead?" Ivy swallowed hard as she stirred the cocoa mix. "How long ago did that happen?"

"A year." Josh's delivery was hollow as he rubbed his thumb against the smooth wood of the table. "She'd been sick for a long time before it happened. My dad was sad but said it was a relief because she wasn't in pain any longer."

Ivy had no idea how to proceed. Thankfully Max stepped in to handle the next round of questioning.

"That sounds awful," Max offered. "Was she in the hospital?"

"At the end. Before that she was at home, but she was always getting sick and they had no idea what was making her that way. She went to the emergency room a lot and was always tired. Before she got sick she was always out doing stuff, like playing tennis and working in her garden. After, though, she didn't do anything but try to get better."

"Well ... I think that's probably a normal reaction," Max said. "How long was she sick?"

"A long time."

"Like ... years?"

Josh nodded. "She was in the hospital for almost a month the last time," he explained. "Dad was there with her whenever he could be, but he had to work because otherwise he wouldn't keep his insurance and he had to keep that. I know because I heard them talking."

Ivy felt sick to her stomach as she carried the hot chocolate to the table. "That's awful, sweetheart. What was wrong with her?"

"The doctors don't know." Josh nodded in thanks as he accepted his mug, his manners ingrained even though most people would've forgotten them given the circumstances. "No one told me a lot, but they often forgot I was around and could listen. It was a medical mystery. That's what they called it. She had a lot of symptoms, but every test they ran came up empty."

"That is absolutely horrible." Ivy tried to picture going through something similar with one of her parents and was utterly wrecked at the possibility. "So, it's just been you and your dad ever since? Do you have any brothers or sisters?"

"No. It's just me." Josh made a slurping sound when he drank his cocoa. "Mom wanted another kid, but then she got sick so it didn't happen."

"That's too bad," Max said. "I wasn't thrilled when my parents added Ivy to the mix, but I grew to love her ... eventually. As embarrassed as I am to admit it, I tried to sell her to the neighbors when I was four. They wouldn't take her."

Even though he was clearly upset, a ghost of a smile haunted Josh's lips. "Did you get in trouble?"

"Yes, although my father actually thought it was funny so it wasn't big trouble or anything." Max kicked back in his chair and crossed his feet at the ankles. "What about aunts and uncles, buddy? Do you have any of those?"

Josh shrugged. "I have an aunt on my mom's side, but I don't know where she lives. It's not close. We never see her. I have an uncle on my dad's side, too, but they don't get along. I think he lives in London, wherever that is."

Ivy didn't find the news heartening. "What about grandparents?"

"Dead."

Of course. It seemed everyone in young Josh's life was gone. "What about family friends?" Ivy prodded gently. "I mean ... who did your parents want you to live with in case something happened to them?"

"I don't know." Josh's eyes misted. "They never said. I don't think they thought this would happen."

"Of course not," Ivy agreed. "No one could've ever seen this happening."

That would make finding a home for Josh all the more difficult, she realized. The poor kid simply could not catch a break.

IT WAS WELL PAST LUNCH time when Jack and Brian made their way to the cottage. Ivy made peanut butter and jelly sandwiches – that was all she had that appealed to a teenager – and Brian and Jack didn't offer any complaints when they settled at the table and she served them the same.

"Thank you, honey," Jack said perfunctorily. "I didn't realize how hungry I was until I walked through the door and smelled whatever it is you're cooking."

"More cookies." Ivy forced a smile that didn't make it all the way to her eyes as she lightly rested her hand on Jack's thigh under the table. It had been a long morning and she needed the tactile contact. "Josh here has quite the appetite, so we tore through everything I set aside for you. Of course, Max helped."

Max grinned when Jack sent him a mock threatening look. "I'm always happy to take cookies off your hands."

"That's why we're making more," Ivy explained.

"That's good." Jack winked at Josh, but the gesture elicited no reaction from the boy. "I don't know anyone who doesn't like the smell of fresh cookies."

"Me either," Brian agreed, his eyes thoughtful as he watched Josh drink his hot cocoa and stare at the table. "How did the conversation go on family members? We need to start making some calls as soon as lunch is over."

"Well, that's the thing," Ivy hedged. "It seems Josh doesn't have any family. His mother is dead and he doesn't have any grandparents or aunts in the area. Well ... maybe one aunt." Ivy launched into the information, keeping her recital brief and to the point. "So, we clearly need to figure something out," she finished. "I told Josh not to worry because you guys would know exactly what to do."

Jack shifted uncomfortably on his chair as he snagged gazes with

Brian. It was true. He knew exactly what to do. It wasn't something Ivy was going to like, though. "We'll call CPS."

"What's that?" Max asked, legitimately curious.

"It's a group of people with the state who help kids in situations like Josh here," Jack replied. "They'll know what to do. This is the sort of situation they were created for."

"But what is it?" Max pressed. "I mean ... what do the letters stand for?"

Jack wasn't keen to answer so he paused before opening his mouth. That allowed Josh time to do it for him.

"Child Protective Services," Josh supplied darkly. "They take kids and put them in a box when they have no parents."

Ivy was absolutely flabbergasted. "That's not what happens."

"It is." Josh's temper flared to life. "I know it is. It happened to a kid in my school. His father got picked up for drunk driving and they put him in jail because it was like the tenth time he'd done it or something. The CPS people came and dragged him out of the school and they put him in a box."

"Is that what he told you?" Brian asked gently.

"We never saw him again," Josh fired back. "That's what another girl who had been taken by CPS told us. I don't want to go in a box." Josh was practically choking on his tears when he turned to Ivy. "Don't let them put me in a box. Please!"

Ivy thought her heart was going to break. "Oh, sweetheart, they're not going to put you in a box." She wrapped her arm around Josh's back to soothe him. "That's just a story that girl told. That's not what they do."

"I don't want to go with them." Josh was adamant. "Can't I stay with you? I mean ... I'll be good. I'll be quiet. You won't hear a peep out of me. I'll even do chores to earn my keep. Can't I please stay with you?"

Ivy wanted to acquiesce simply to stop the boy from crying, but she knew better than jumping the gun on something this serious. Instead, to buy time, she rubbed his back and turned to Jack. "We'll figure something out, right?"

Jack blinked several times in rapid succession when he realized Ivy was putting him on the hot seat. *Did she really think they would be able to take a young teenager into their home out of the blue?* "Honey, um ... ." Jack stumbled over his words and was thankful when Brian smoothly stepped in to take the decision out of his hands.

"Ivy, you know that Josh can't just move in here and pretend that nothing happened," Brian supplied. "He has to be processed by the state. There's nothing we can do about that. It's state law and we're beholden to it."

Ivy was nothing if not obstinate. "But ... can't we work out something with them? I mean, you guys are cops. Can't you force them to see things our way?"

"No." Brian didn't back down and Jack was grateful for it. The last thing Jack wanted was to be the bad guy in Josh's story. What Ivy was asking was ridiculous, though. "We have rules to follow, Ivy. We don't have a choice in the matter."

Ivy's eyes glittered with tears when she met Jack's conflicted gaze. "Are you sure?"

"Honey, I wish I could give you a different answer." Jack chose his words carefully. "Josh needs to be with people who can help him. We're not those people."

"You don't know that," Josh challenged. "I don't want to be taken away from Ivy. She's the only one who cares."

The look on Ivy's face was murderous when Jack opened his mouth to argue further. She wasn't going to take whatever he had to say well. There was nothing he could do about that, though. She'd backed him into a corner and they both knew it.

"We're going to make sure you're well taken care of, Josh," Jack promised. "It's going to be okay. We're going to do right by you."

It was a lame offering, but it was all he had. One look at Ivy's face told Jack it wasn't going to be enough.

"We're going to do right by you," he repeated. "You have my word on it."

Four

Jack was annoyed when he woke the next morning and found Ivy on her side of the bed. Usually, and it was one of his favorite things about waking up with his feisty partner, she was almost on top of him when he woke most mornings.

She rested her head on his shoulder, her hand on his heart, and proceeded to drool throughout the night. She also poked her bare feet out of the covers no matter the temperature and made sighing noises in his ear that he'd started to associate with soothing white noise. Since she was angry with him about turning Josh over to Child Protective Services, none of those things happened the previous evening. Er, well, except for the feet. Jack lifted his head to make sure and scowled when he saw her painted toenails gleaming under the morning light spilling through the bedroom window.

He flicked his eyes to Ivy, who had her back to him, and weighed the best way to smooth things over. Jack didn't consider himself one of the great talkers in the world, but he had a very good idea exactly how he saw things going and he had no intention of backing down until Ivy forgave him.

With that in mind, Jack rolled until his chest was pressed against Ivy's back. He felt her stir, melt into him for a second, and he recognized the moment she remembered she was angry with him and tried to pull away. That's when he tightened his grip on her and lowered his mouth to the ridge of her ear.

"Oh, there's no escape, honey." He kissed the delicate skin on her neck. "You're not leaving this bed until you forgive me."

Ivy wasn't one of those women who woke with a smile on her face – unless the strenuous activity from the previous evening was so outstanding and memorable she had no choice – but she was in a particularly vile mood this morning. "Let me go."

"No."

Ivy slapped at Jack's hand, frustrated. "I said to let me go!"

"No." Jack was firm as he sobered. "I'm not letting you go until we talk about this. I'm not happy with what happened last night."

Ivy's eyebrows practically flew off her forehead. "You're not happy with what happened last night? I can pretty much guarantee that Josh is a lot unhappier."

Jack heaved out a frustrated sigh and released Ivy's wriggling form. He was happy when she didn't immediately race out of the bed to get away from him, but he knew he was in for an argument when she rolled to face him. There was fire in her eyes.

"I didn't send that boy with the CPS folks to be mean to you or him," he started. "You know that. I felt bad for him. We still had to follow procedure."

"He was traumatized."

"And so were you," Jack surmised. "You bonded with him because you found him and you couldn't stop your heart from breaking because of the story he told. I get it ... and I'm sorry. You'll never know how sorry.

"That doesn't mean I had a choice in the matter," he continued. "If I tried to keep that kid and let you fawn over him I would've lost my job and we both would've possibly ended up in jail. Is that what you wanted?"

Ivy was mortified by the question. "Of course not."

"Then what do you want from me?" Jack challenged. "What magic did you expect me to weave so you could keep that kid when he belonged with the state workers?"

Ivy licked her lips, clearly caught off guard by Jack's tone. "Stop yelling at me," she said after a beat, dragging a restless hand through her snarled hair. "I don't like it when you yell at me."

"Yeah? I don't like it when you treat me like dirt over something I can't change."

Ivy narrowed her eyes to dangerous slits. "I didn't treat you like dirt."

"You certainly didn't treat me like the man you're going to marry," Jack challenged. "You didn't treat me like a human being who has feelings, or a good cop who did the right thing."

Even though she was used to sticking her foot in her mouth on a regular basis, Ivy recognized when she'd stepped over a line. Jack's demeanor told her exactly that. "I didn't mean to hurt your feelings." She licked her lips as she debated how to proceed. "That's the last thing I wanted."

"Apology accepted." Jack took her by surprise when he slipped his arm around her waist and tugged her to him. "We should make up the proper way so we don't jinx anything. You can start by kissing me now. Don't be afraid to use your tongue."

Ivy's mouth dropped open as incredulity washed over her. "You ... we ... I'm not kissing you!" She slapped her hand to his chest to keep him at bay. "You totally tricked me. You pretended I hurt your feelings so you could cop a feel."

Jack's grin was impish as he regarded her. "That's not entirely true, honey," he countered. "I wasn't lying about not being happy. I much prefer waking to find you wrapped around me. It's comfortable. I used to think I would smother if I slept with another individual like that in a bed – which is only one of the reasons I didn't like having a serious girlfriend – but now I can't remember a time when I was comfortable sleeping any other way."

Ivy glared. "That's not going to work on me. I know what you're doing."

Jack ignored the statement and barreled forward. "I didn't sleep well because I didn't have you in my arms," he offered. "I also didn't sleep well because I knew you were upset. I don't ever want you to be upset."

Despite herself, Ivy found her cold reserve melting. Jack had a way about him. She was determined to keep her anger front and center no matter how adorable she found him. "I ... ."

Jack shook his head to cut her off. "I love you. That's the one thing I know with absolute certainty. I don't like it when you're angry with me. I know that, too. I also did the right thing when it came to Josh. I couldn't let you keep him no matter how your heart broke at the prospect of sending him away. You are not trained to deal with a kid in mourning and Josh needs specific care going forward."

Instead of fire, Ivy met Jack's statement with morose resignation. "I know." Her voice was barely a whisper. "He was begging, though. He was so afraid."

"Oh, I know." Jack pulled her tighter against him, internally sighing when she stopped fighting and rested her head on his chest. His hands were calm and steady as they rubbed her back. "Honey, I don't ever want to tell you no, but I didn't have a choice last night. You know that, right?"

Ivy mutely nodded, a tear spilling on her cheek.

"Oh, don't do that." Jack swiped at the tear. "I hate that."

"I'm sorry." Ivy sniffled a bit but managed to pull herself together. "I didn't mean to jump all over you. When that man showed up from the state and physically removed Josh from the house even though he was sobbing ... and begging ... and crying ... ."

"You fell apart," Jack finished, pressing a soft kiss to her forehead. "That's because you're a freaking warrior and wanted to fight for that boy from the moment you saw him. There's only so much you can do, honey. You can't be everything he needs. You're not equipped for that."

"I know." Ivy *did* know that. She understood Jack was right. That didn't change the fact that she was traumatized when Josh was practically ripped away from her and dragged toward a van for transportation. "You heard his story, though. He's all alone. I mean ... what's going to happen to him?"

"I don't know." Jack opted for honesty. "The first order of business today is tracking down family members for Josh."

"You heard him. He doesn't have anybody."

"That he knows of," Jack corrected. "It sounds to me like the kid had a rough year. To lose his mother the way he did to a terrible illness and then to have his father gunned down in front of him that way, it's a lot for a kid to deal with. He might not have been thinking clearly."

"Yeah. I guess." Ivy rubbed at her red-rimmed eyes, the gesture somehow childlike and innocent to the point that it tugged on Jack's heartstrings. "How much is he expected to go through?"

The real question, Jack silently muttered in his head, was how much was Ivy expected to go through. "I'll keep you updated on what we have. I promise." He nestled her face against his chest. "We had to wait for the state police tech team to finish last night, but we're on this hard starting today. I promise we'll come up with some answers."

"Okay." Ivy made the sniffling sound again.

"Honey, are you trying to kill me?" Jack wrapped his arms tightly around her slim back. "You know I can't stand it when you cry."

"I'm not crying."

"You sound like you're crying."

"I have something in my eye."

"Tears?"

"I'm okay, Jack." Ivy's expression was rueful as she pulled back, her eyes glassy but resigned. "I'm sorry I was mean to you. I just ... I felt horrible. You know if I feel horrible that you have to feel it, too."

Jack didn't want to encourage bad behavior with a smile, but he couldn't stop himself. She was too adorable for words. "Well, honey, I'm happy to commiserate with you. However, I don't like it when you take things out on me that I can't control."

"Yeah. That wasn't fair." Ivy ran her index finger down his cheek. "Do you want me to make it up to you?"

Jack's lips curved when he picked up on what she was offering. "Well, we have an hour before the painters arrive and I have to leave for work. What did you have in mind?"

For the first time all morning, Ivy mustered a legitimate smile. "Why don't I just show you? It will probably lose something in the telling."

"That sounds like a fabulous idea."

. . .

JACK HAD AN EXTRA spring in his step when he let himself into the office he shared with Brian. The office aide, Ava Moffett, happened to be delivering reports when he arrived and her eyes gleamed with warm welcome when she caught sight of Jack.

"I was starting to think you weren't going to show up." Ava was relatively young, in her late twenties, and she'd been rather overt when displaying her interest in Jack since he landed in Shadow Lake a year before. As the chief of police's daughter, Ava thought she was a catch even though Jack did his best to convince her otherwise whenever she threw herself at him.

"Good morning, Ava." Jack met Brian's amused eyes as he headed to his desk. "What? Why do you look so happy?"

"I was just about to ask you that same question," Brian drawled, leaning back in his chair. "You're all ... glow-y ... this morning."

"That is true, Jack," Ava said as she planted her rear end on the corner of Jack's desk and looked him up and down. "You're radiating from within today. That must mean you're in a good mood."

"I have nothing to complain about," Jack clarified. "I don't know what 'radiating from within' means, but it doesn't sound horrible so I'm fine with doing it."

Brian snorted, legitimately amused. "I wasn't sure which Jack I'd be getting this morning. Given Ivy's mood when Josh was taken away last night, I figured you were in for a rough one. I'm guessing you two made up."

Jack's cheeks burned under his partner's studied gaze. "I don't kiss and tell."

"No one would want to own up to kissing Ivy Morgan and telling about it," Ava muttered loud enough for Jack to hear the words.

"Oh, don't get me wrong, I have no problem singing to the rooftop about Ivy," Jack shot back. "As for this morning, though, what we did was private."

"Oh, you're such a schmuck." Brian rolled his eyes and stared at the ceiling. "You know I don't like hearing about this stuff. To me she'll always be the little girl in pigtails who her father carted around with him everywhere for a time. She handed out lollipops to people she liked."

"To me she'll always be the weird girl no one liked in high school," Ava offered. "There's a reason for that. Kids know when someone is frightening and not worth their time."

Jack furrowed his brow as his dark gaze landed on Ava. "Is there a reason you're hanging around our office today?"

"There is." Ava bobbed her head. "I dropped off a report for Brian. It's supposed to be very important."

"It's from the state police," Brian volunteered as he flipped open the file in question. "They had K-9 units and tech teams out in the woods all day yesterday."

"I know." Jack turned serious. "I could see the cars going up and down the road from the bay window in the living room. Ivy wasn't talking to me, so I had nothing better to do than watch traffic."

Brian chuckled. "You two are a little co-dependent for my comfort level."

"I think we're just co-dependent enough," Jack countered.

"And I think she cast a spell on you or something," Ava groused in a low voice. "Everyone knows she did something to get you to focus on her while ignoring everyone else ... like me."

Jack managed to tamp down on his fury, but just barely. "Is there a reason you're still here, Ava?"

"What?" She adopted an innocent expression and pressed her hand to her chest. "Why would you possibly ask that? I'm here to help."

"You're here to give me indigestion," Jack corrected. "Since Ivy cooked a big breakfast before sending me on my way, I think the heartburn you're going to generate is going to be something fierce. I'm telling you right now, you don't want to push things this morning."

"I never push things." Ava's smile was serene. "I'm a giving soul. I was merely explaining why you made a big mistake when you decided to hitch your wagon to Ivy Morgan."

"Since I love her and she makes me happy, I'm going to go with my first assumption that you're jealous and a terrible individual," Jack countered. "I don't care what you think about Ivy. Your opinion has no bearing on me."

Ava let loose with a disgusted growl in the back of her throat.

"You'll change your mind when you finally see for yourself that I'm right."

"Well, until then, I would appreciate it if you didn't mention Ivy. Not even one word." Jack was firm. "I'll come to you when I've come to the conclusion that I've made a mistake. Until then ... stuff it."

"Fine." Ava's eyes flashed with annoyance as she stood. "I'm guessing you're going to be coming to me sooner rather than later."

Jack snorted. "And I'm guessing you're going to be waiting for a long time and end up bitter and disappointed. That doesn't bother me because you're already the bitter sort. Now ... go." He made a small shooing motion with his hand and focused on Brian. "Anything in that report we can work with?"

"Not really." Brian was grim as he handed it to his partner. "They searched the woods for hours last night. The dogs didn't find a trail. They didn't find footprints ... or an abandoned gun ... or tire tracks along the road that would suggest another vehicle was parked there and someone took off in a hurry."

Jack's heart sank. "So, you're saying we have nothing to go on?"

"Absolutely nothing." Brian rubbed the back of his neck as he stared at the ceiling. "I guess that means we're going to have to do things the old-fashioned way."

"Meaning we start with family and close friends and work our way out," Jack surmised. "The problem with that is, Abraham Masters didn't have a lot of family. We'd better hope we make some headway with his friends."

"That's the plan." Brian slowly got to his feet. "I think we should head over to Bellaire right away. We're probably going to spend the entire afternoon questioning people."

"Okay." Jack was resigned as he followed his partner. "We have to do whatever is necessary to find answers. I promised Ivy we would do our best."

Brian paused by the door. "Speaking of Ivy, how is she doing? Is she better now that she's had some time to calm down?"

"No. She cried. She's still traumatized by Josh being taken away."

"She's going to let it go, though, right? She's not going to get involved in this, is she?"

Jack was exasperated as he snagged his partner's gaze. "She said she wasn't going to cause problems."

"Do you believe her?"

"No." Jack made an exaggerated face. "You've met her. She's going to be all over this until we have answers. She made a big show of saying she was going to work at the nursery today, but I've got twenty bucks that says she's already on her way to the children's home to visit Josh."

"Ugh." Brian rubbed his forehead. "She's going to be trouble if she gets involved in this."

"She's already involved ... and she's already trouble."

"Well, at least we know what to expect." Brian brightened a bit. "Hey, given some of her ... talents ... maybe she can help us. We can't rule it out."

"That's the only reason I haven't put my foot down with her."

Brian's expression shifted to rampant amusement. "That's the only reason, huh? It has nothing to do with you being a big puddle of goo where she's concerned, does it?"

"Not in the least."

"I don't believe you."

"That's good. I don't believe me either." Jack was rueful. "She's going to do what she wants and I'm going to let her. We all know it."

Brian barked out a laugh as he clapped Jack's shoulder. "At least you're aware of your limitations. Believe it or not, that's something."

Jack wasn't sure what to believe. "Let's just get to it. The faster we get answers, the more likely Ivy is not to find trouble."

"That sounds like a plan."

Five

Jack knew Ivy well. She did indeed head to the children's home the minute he left the house. She took enough time to shower and change, but then she made a beeline for the facility. She knew where it was because she donated her time there for various fundraisers throughout the years.

The facility was locked, a pass card needed to gain entrance. Ivy pressed the button to call for an attendant and patiently waited to see who would show up. She was relieved when she found a familiar face waiting for her.

"Hey, Dana."

Dana Wolfe-Leeds was a former Shadow Lake classmate. She graduated two years before Ivy, but she'd never been antagonistic toward the younger girl. Ivy couldn't say that about a lot of people. Since she was different even then, she was often ostracized. Children tend to pick out the one individual who doesn't fit nicely into a group and peck him or her to death. Dana was never that way. Ivy occasionally ran into her in the years since they both graduated and their conversations were always friendly and amiable.

"Hey, Ivy." Dana was understandably confused as she looked over the visitor. Ivy wore one of her typical ankle-length skirts and a peasant blouse and she had a bag of what looked to be freshly-baked cookies in her hand. "Do you have an appointment or something?"

"No." Ivy had practiced this conversation in her head for the entire drive between Shadow Lake and Bellaire. She could only hope Dana would take pity on her sad tale and let her in. "I'm here to see Josh Masters."

Dana's eyebrows hopped. "What? You can't just wander in here to see one of our kids."

"I was the one who found him in the woods yesterday," Ivy prodded, keeping her pleading smile in place even though she felt mildly guilty about exaggerating. Josh was the one who found her, after all. Still, she was desperate to see the boy. "I was with him for hours. I don't want to steal him or anything. I just want to visit with him. Look, I brought cookies."

Dana was a nice woman, but she wasn't a pushover. She read Ivy's intent from the start. "Are you supposed to be here?"

"I ... what do you mean?" Ivy feigned ignorance. "No one said I couldn't be here."

"Uh-huh." Dana remained unconvinced. "If I call Brian Nixon or Jack Harker in Shadow Lake and ask them if you're supposed to be here, what are they going to say?"

Ivy's lips turned down in a scowl. "Why would you possibly do that?"

Dana snorted, more amused than annoyed. "That's what I thought." She tilted her head to the side as she regarded the pink-haired siren. "This goes against the rules. We're not supposed to let outsiders visit with our charges, especially in situations like Josh is facing."

Ivy sensed a weakening in Dana's countenance. "He cried when they pulled him away from me at that cottage. He was upset, which upset me. I promise not to stay too long. I just want to see him."

Dana heaved out a sigh and pushed open the door so Ivy could enter. She waited until the door was locked and securely shut behind them – she tested it twice to make sure it held before leading Ivy inside – to continue speaking. "I'm going to allow this but only because Josh seems like an extremely sad individual right now."

Ivy brightened considerably. "Thank you."

"Don't thank me yet." Dana held up her hand to still Ivy before the enthusiastic woman could get ahead of herself. "I have to go in with you."

"I'm fine with that."

"Josh might not welcome you with open arms either," Dana cautioned. "He's a bit ... irritated ... with the situation. He feels as if we're holding him hostage here and he doesn't like it one bit."

"I'll talk to him," Ivy promised. "I don't know him that well, but we bonded yesterday. I'm invested in making sure he gets the best possible outcome."

"That's exactly why I'm giving you the chance," Dana admitted. "We've been having a rough time with Josh since last night. He's morose and sad. No one expects differently because he lost his father. He's making things more difficult than they have to be."

"That's why I brought the cookies." Ivy shook the bag for emphasis. "I'm sure he'll talk to me."

"I hope so." Dana grabbed the bag from Ivy and opened it, snagging a cookie before handing it back. "You bribed me with this cookie for entry if anyone asks. Anyone who knows me understands I can be bought with chocolate. They don't even judge me for it."

Ivy beamed at the woman. "I think we all can be bought with chocolate under the right circumstances."

PAUL RUNYON WAS THE medical examiner on duty when Jack and Brian entered the examination room shortly after eleven. They were on a mission for answers and their investigation started with the body on the gurney.

"Hey." Paul was expecting the detectives so he couldn't muster surprise at their appearance. "I knew you guys would show up. I figured it would be after lunch, though."

"Do you need more time?" Jack asked.

Paul shook his head. "No. I'm pretty much done here. I found a few surprises, although I'm not sure if you'll think that's a good thing."

"Lay it on us," Brian instructed, folding his arms over his chest as he leaned against the nearby counter. "What do you have?"

"Well, first off, Abraham Masters was in pretty good shape," Paul volunteered. "His heart and lungs were functioning well and I couldn't find any underlying medical conditions that would've caused him immediate worry. He was fit and healthy for his age."

"We didn't think he died of natural causes," Jack pointed out.

"I know. Hold your horses." Paul made an exasperated face, his eyes twinkling. He enjoyed messing with law enforcement officers whenever the mood hit. "He was shot in the chest at close range, his ventricular artery basically severed. He didn't linger. He died quickly."

"How quickly?" Brian asked.

"Less than a minute."

"Okay, that's fast." Brian shifted from one foot to the other. "You said he was shot at close range. That seems unnecessary for a rifle. Can you think of a reason why someone would need to be close in those circumstances?"

"Rifle?" Paul furrowed his brow. "It wasn't a rifle."

Jack stilled. "Are you sure?"

"I'm positive." Paul grabbed the report he was writing up and handed it to Jack. "The state boys are going to have to do a ballistics match, but it was definitely a handgun. I can tell from the angle more than anything else. A rifle would've been looking down. Whoever did this had unsteady hands and the gun tilted up."

Jack and Brian exchanged a quick look, something Paul didn't miss.

"What's wrong?" Paul asked, leaning forward. "Is that not right? Are you suggesting I'm wrong?"

"We didn't say anything." Jack licked his lips as he ran the scenario through his head. "We have a witness to this shooting, and he said that the assailant had a hunting rifle."

Paul stared at Abraham's open chest cavity for a long beat before slowly starting to shake his head. "No, that's not right. The grooves on a rifle and handgun are similar but not exact. I'm positive the slug I dug out belonged to a handgun."

"Who takes a handgun into the woods, though?" Brian challenged.

"I mean ... that doesn't make a lot of sense. If you go into the woods to shoot, you take a rifle. A handgun is for home protection."

"And concealed carry," Paul pointed out. "Maybe whoever your shooter is carried the gun for protection and was startled."

"By a guy picking mushrooms in the woods with his kid?" Brian wasn't convinced. "There's something off about this."

"Maybe Josh was confused when he told us the story yesterday," Jack suggested. "Maybe he had trouble remembering things because he was in shock."

"Or maybe he's not telling us everything," Brian countered. "Maybe he recognized who shot his father and isn't saying anything because he's afraid that individual could be coming after him."

"If he did lie, he's not going to own up to it right away," Jack pointed out. "He's going to stick to his story because he's afraid. You saw him yesterday, the kid is definitely afraid."

"Yeah." Brian thoughtfully stroked his chin. "We need him to open up, but he's only going to do it with someone he trusts."

Jack knew exactly what his partner was going to suggest before Brian opened his mouth a second time. "Don't ask me to involve Ivy in this."

"You said yourself that she was going to involve herself," Brian pointed out. "She's probably at the children's home right now trying to see him."

"She can't get in," Jack pointed out. "I don't care how persuasive she is, no one in their right mind is going to let her wander around the children's home and spend time with a traumatized kid."

Brian snorted, amusement flitting through his eyes. "You're the one who says you can't say no to her."

"That's different. We're getting married."

"How is it different?" Brian challenged. "She had to snag you from the start and you never wanted to tell her no. You've simply given up now. What makes you think you're the only one?"

"It's true," Paul said sagely. "I've been trying to get Ivy Morgan to say yes to me for years. I never would've said no to her. I was crushed when you came to town and snapped her up. I thought I still had a chance if I played things right. It never happened, though."

"And it's never going to happen." Jack extended a warning finger as he glanced between faces. Calling Ivy was the last thing he wanted to do, but he didn't see where he had much choice. He heaved out a resigned sigh after a few moments. "Fine. I'll ask her to talk to the kid. I refuse to push her, though. She's already too invested in this."

"I don't want her to press him," Brian said. "I want her to gain his trust so he wants to tell her. He's living in fear right now. We can't even look in the right place until he snaps out of it."

"I'm sure Ivy will love having a mission." Jack dug in his pocket for his phone. "She's thrilled when I include her in stuff."

"I'd love to give her a mission," Paul noted, causing Jack to scowl.

"Don't make me thump you," Jack warned.

"It might be worth it if Ivy plays nurse to me." Paul winked to let Jack know he was kidding. "As for the rest of the autopsy, there's nothing else of note. I'll have a full report on your desk by the end of the day."

"That's something at least."

JOSH WAS IN A FOUL mood when Dana led Ivy into the recreation room at the back of the house. Even though the facility was full of children, Josh was the only one in the room. Ivy was unnerved by the silence as she crossed to the young teenager.

"Hey, buddy."

Josh jerked up his head at the sound of her voice and instantly hopped to his feet. His eyes were red-rimmed from crying, dark circles puffing out beneath them, and the look of hope on his face was enough to shake Ivy to the core. "Did you come to take me back home with you?"

Ivy forced her smile to stay in place even as she started shaking her head. "I can't take you with me. Jack explained all of that last night."

Josh's expression turned dour. "Then why did you even bother to come here?"

"Because I wanted to see you." Ivy tried to keep the boy's obvious fury from affecting her. He had a right to his feelings, she reminded herself. If she lost both her parents in a year's time – one to unthinkable violence right in front of her – she was fairly certain she wouldn't be a bright star in a cloudy night either. "I was worried about you."

Josh stared into her eyes for a long time, his expression never changing.

"I wanted to see how you were doing," Ivy continued. "You're all I could think about."

"I bet your boyfriend hates that," Josh grumbled after a beat. "Did he try to stop you from coming to see me?"

"No." Ivy shook her head. "I know you and Jack didn't get off on the best footing yesterday, but he's a good man."

"A good man wouldn't have sent me here."

Ivy briefly flicked her eyes to Dana and got a shrug in response to the unasked question. Clearly Dana didn't have ideas for perking up Josh either. "Jack is a police officer," Ivy explained, choosing her words carefully. "He has to follow certain rules. He doesn't always like those rules, but he doesn't have a choice. He can't pick and choose which ones to follow and which ones to ignore."

"He just didn't want me spending time with you," Josh muttered, using his thumbnail to scratch at something only he could see on the tabletop. "He was jealous because he thought I was going to take up too much of your time."

Despite the serious nature of the situation, Ivy had to bite back a smile. "Well, Jack has nothing to be jealous about. I honestly don't think that's the case. Still, I'm sorry how things turned out. I didn't like letting them take you, but I didn't have a choice either."

"And you're not here to cut me loose?" Josh asked forlornly.

"I can't do that," Ivy said. "It's not allowed."

"Then why bother coming here and getting my hopes up?" Josh crossed his arms over his chest. "I can't believe you did this to me. I thought you were going to take me out, at least for a little while. Instead I'm stuck here."

"Well ... ." Ivy looked to Dana for a moment, something occurring to her. "Stay here a second, Josh." She handed him the bag of cookies and motioned for Dana to move across the room with her.

Dana was already prepared for Ivy's world-class charm to be on full display before the pink-haired woman even opened her mouth. "Whatever you're thinking, the answer is no."

Ivy held up her hand to quiet the woman. "Just hear me out."

"No."

"Please?"

"Ugh." Dana made a face. "I knew allowing you in here was a bad idea. You're going to turn this into a thing, aren't you? No cookie is worth this. I'm just warning you now."

Ivy didn't let the diatribe knock her back. "That cookie was awesome and you know it."

"It's not worth losing my job."

"Why do you have to lose your job?" Ivy was earnest. "I have an idea. If you need me to fill out paperwork and stuff, I get it. If you need to clear it with a supervisor, I get that, too. I want you to at least consider it, though."

"I am not letting you take that kid home." Dana was firm. "Besides the fact that Jack would have a heart attack if he turned up at the cottage and found you adopted a kid without his knowledge, you're not licensed to be a caregiver."

"I don't want to be a caregiver," Ivy countered. "Jack and I aren't ready to take on a kid. I'm not an idiot."

"Oh." Dana had the grace to be abashed. "If you don't want the kid, what do you want?"

"I want you to clear an outing," Ivy replied without hesitation. "I want you to allow me to take Josh for the afternoon, not for the rest of his life."

"Where do you want to take him?"

"Not far. Just to the nursery."

Dana knit her eyebrows, confused. "But ... why?"

"Because I don't think it's healthy for him to be here," Ivy answered. "He's not happy in this place. He thinks he's being caged. If I take him to the nursery he'll be out in the open and able to get some fresh air. My father will be there and between the two of us we'll keep him busy helping us all afternoon. We're getting ready for the big planting season. We'll have so many customers he won't be able to think of anything but helping."

"I don't know." Despite her misgivings, Dana found she wasn't completely opposed to the idea. "It's actually not a terrible thought, but I'm not sure I can clear it without a tour of your nursery."

"Well ... why not come with us?" Ivy suggested, her mind working overtime. "I can leave ahead of you and tell my father what's going on. You can meet us there. You can look over the nursery. If you don't think it's safe, you can hang out for an hour and pretend that's all you had planned. If you do think it's safe, you can leave him with us for a bit and I'll bring him back."

Dana blinked several times in rapid succession. "You could talk a pirate out of his booty, couldn't you?"

Ivy smiled. She knew she'd already won. "So ... you'll at least give it a shot?"

"I'll give it a shot, but only because I think it's the best thing for Josh," Dana confirmed. "He was lifeless until you showed up. I'm willing to try anything."

"Great." Ivy let loose a relieved sigh and smiled at Josh. "Do you want to tell him or should I?"

"I'll handle that. We don't want to get ahead of ourselves until I'm sure he can stay at the nursery. If we tell him he can go and then yank him back, that will do more harm than good."

"Good point."

"I'm full of them."

"Yeah." Ivy handed over the bag of cookies. "Go nuts. You've earned them."

"Ugh. I'm really starting to dislike you right now. You're going to be terrible for my waistline."

"You look like a model. Don't worry about your waistline."

"I'm starting to like you a little more," Dana conceded. "Let's go talk to him and see what he says. We'll cushion the trip as a group outing initially. If he doesn't want to go, though, I'm not going to make him."

"Deal."

Six

"You want me to do what?"

Jack called Ivy when she was on her way to the nursery, and when he explained what they needed from her she wasn't keen on the request.

"I want you to get him talking about what happened in the woods," Jack replied, refusing to back down. "If you can get him to talk about his family a little more, that would be great, too."

Ivy kept her focus on the road, which was thankfully empty, and drummed her fingers on the steering wheel as she debated how to answer. "I'm not sure I'm comfortable with that, Jack," she said finally. "I'm the only one he seems to trust right now."

"And that's why I'm asking you to do it. I figured you were probably on your way to the home, right? You don't have to push him, but if you could direct the conversation in a specific manner, it may help us figure out what's going on."

"Actually, I've already been to the children's home."

Jack was silent for a beat on the other end of the call.

"I'm on my way back to Shadow Lake now," Ivy added.

"You didn't stay very long." Jack struggled to contain his surprise. "Couldn't you get in to see him?"

"As a matter of fact, I got in to see him right away," Ivy replied. "I happened to know the woman answering the door. We went to high school together, although she was two years ahead of me."

"Oh, well, I figured you wouldn't have trouble getting inside because you're you."

"I also bribed her with fresh chocolate chip cookies."

"My chocolate chip cookies?"

"They're not yours any longer," Ivy replied smoothly. "I needed them for a bribe, so I took them."

"You made them for me."

"I'll make you more later."

"Fine." Jack blew out a sigh. Haggling over cookies was going to get him nowhere. "So, what happened? Was he upset about last night?"

"He's definitely upset. He blames you for bullying me into letting the CPS people take him."

"Ivy, if we're going to get into another fight about this, it's going to have to wait until later. I can't have this discussion again. I thought we talked things out."

"We did, and I understand your point of view," Ivy supplied. "Josh is too young to understand. He's very upset by everything that's happened. I can't say I blame him. He's an orphan and he was shoved into a group home last night. That would be unsettling for anyone."

"I agree. I guess that means he kicked you out, huh?"

"No, he did not kick me out. Dana and I talked, though, and we agreed that perhaps keeping him in the home wasn't such a hot idea."

The hair on the back of Jack's neck stood up. "Oh, please tell me you didn't somehow sweet talk that woman into giving you custody of that kid. If you did, we're going to have a problem."

"First off, if I did, you would have to deal with it because it would mean I was doing what I thought was right," Ivy shot back. "Secondly, that's not what I did so you can chill out."

Jack took a cleansing breath. "Well, at least that's one thing we won't have to fight about."

"I didn't do it solely for you," Ivy offered. "I did it for both of us. We're not ready to take care of a kid with Josh's emotional needs. I know you think I'm all heart and no brains, but I'm honestly not a complete and total idiot."

"I think you have a huge heart and your brains are fine," Jack clarified. "In fact, I happen to love every part of you, including that mouth of yours even though it tends to get ahead of you sometimes."

"I think that was an insult and compliment all rolled into one."

"It was merely the truth," Jack countered. "If you weren't kicked out of the home and you're on your way back to Shadow Lake, what happened?"

"I talked Dana into allowing Josh to visit the nursery for the afternoon," Ivy replied, opting to stick to the truth. "She's driving him over and once she ascertains the facility is safe she's going to leave him with Dad and me for a few hours and then I'm going to drive him back."

Jack didn't say a word, which was the opposite of the reaction Ivy expected.

"If you're going to yell at me about this," Ivy continued. "I would prefer you do it now. I don't want to carry the dread around with me all day."

"I'm not going to yell at you," Jack said after a moment of silent contemplation. "I actually think it's a good idea."

His admission floored her. "You do?"

"I do. This will allow you to spend time with Josh in a relaxed setting and possibly get him to talk. The story he told doesn't make any sense given the evidence we've collected. My guess is that he knows who killed his father but is terrified to admit it."

"Oh." Ivy didn't know what to make of the statement. "Why wouldn't he tell us? I mean ... I get being afraid. Wouldn't you want to make sure the person who killed your father was put away for life?"

"I would, but we don't know what Josh was thinking when he made his escape," Jack noted. "He could've panicked and told the killer that he wouldn't tell anyone what happened if he let him go. Maybe that's weighing on him. The truth is, I don't want to push the kid so hard he curls up in a ball and refuses to talk to anyone."

"You just want me to push him."

"I don't want that," Jack countered. "I want you to spend time with him, get him talking. We need more information about his family, too.

We're running searches, but the pickings are slim. We've found a step-grandmother and an aunt who are in the area. We're going to be talking to both of them."

"Do you think they might take Josh?"

"I don't know, honey. We haven't even talked to them yet. I can't answer that question."

"I know." Ivy momentarily felt guilty about putting too much pressure on Jack. He'd barely started working the case. "I'll do my best to get him talking, but I'm not going to push him if I think it will damage him. I'm going to play it by ear."

"That's all I ask."

Ivy could practically see Jack smiling through the phone. "What are you thinking?"

"That I love you."

"I love you, too, but that's not what you were thinking."

"I was thinking that I want you to be safe when you take Josh back to the home," Jack admitted. "I doubt very much our killer is going to expect that you would take the boy to the nursery. In fact, that's the exact opposite of anything I would expect if I were in that position. The children's home is another story. Keep your eyes open for strange vehicles when you drop him off."

"I will. I'm always careful."

Jack snorted, disdain evident. "Honey, you're never careful. I've learned to live with that. Be alert for me, though, okay? We still have no idea what we're dealing with here."

"I promise to be alert."

"I'll see you for dinner," Jack said. "I'll be in touch if I get more information."

"Me, too."

"I'll see you as soon as I can."

"I'll be waiting with fresh cookies if I can pull it off."

"And that's only one reason you're my favorite person in the world."

MICHAEL MORGAN WAS WORKING behind the front cash register when Dana arrived with Josh. He knew what to expect thanks to a brief explanation from Ivy, but he met the boy's stern countenance with a wide smile despite the grief that he figured was weighing down the poor child.

"Hello, Dana. It's been a long time."

Dana grinned when she saw him. She was familiar with Michael – like everyone in Shadow Lake was – and she'd always found him to be a pleasant conversationalist. "Hello, Mr. Morgan. I wasn't sure you were back from Florida after your winter break until Ivy mentioned it earlier in the day."

"Please, call me Michael." He gripped the woman's hand and gave it a firm shake before focusing on the boy. "We've only been back for a little bit. I'm always eager to get out of the brutal Michigan winters, but I'm always ready to come back, too, because I love a Michigan spring."

"I think you do things the right way," Dana said. "Eventually I would love to leave this place for the winter and come back for spring, summer, and fall, too. That's the best way to do things."

"I agree, for the most part." Michael's eyes were thoughtful as they roamed Josh's face. The boy appeared disinterested in the conversation, but Michael was convinced it was a rather unconvincing act. "This year was particularly hard for Luna to be away," he said, referring to his wife. "We knew Jack was going to propose to Ivy before we left and it was pure torture for Luna not to be present for it."

"Oh, I didn't even think about the timing of that," Dana said. "I was actually surprised when I heard they got engaged so quickly. It seems like just yesterday that Jack arrived in town and all the eligible women started vrooming their engines trying to get his attention."

Michael snickered, amusement lighting his eyes. "Yes, well, I happen to think they're a good match. They fight quite a bit but that keeps the fires burning. They like to make up." Michael hunkered down a bit so he could look Josh in the face. He was tall, like Max, and that often put people off. "I understand you spent some time with my kids yesterday."

Josh made a face as he looked Michael up and down. "And who are your kids?"

"Mr. Morgan is Max and Ivy's father," Dana explained. "He's a nice guy. You should be polite."

Josh glanced between the woman admonishing him and the man trying so hard to appease him and ultimately shrugged his shoulders. "Sorry. I'm just sick of people asking me questions and treating me like I'm slow or something. It's getting old."

"I can see that." If Michael was bothered by Josh's tone, he didn't show it. "You've been through a lot."

"Let me guess, you're going to make me feel better," Josh drawled. "No offense, sir, but I don't think that's possible."

"We didn't bring you here to make you feel better," Ivy announced, taking Josh by surprise when she appeared in the space behind him. The boy clearly didn't sense her invading his space, but he was thrilled at the sight of her and broke out in a relieved smile.

"If you didn't bring me here to make me feel better, why did you bring me here?"

"To put you to work, of course." Ivy's grin was wide and just a little bit sloppy. "It's the spring season here and that means we have a lot to do. I thought you and I would work in the greenhouse today. How does that sound?"

Josh followed Ivy's finger as she pointed at the building in question. "That looks familiar. I ... think we were here yesterday."

Ivy didn't want to dwell on that, so she simply nodded. "This is my nursery. I own it. It's close to my cottage. We're going to be in the greenhouse, not in the woods."

For a brief moment, fear clouded Josh's eyes. "Are we ... safe?"

"Absolutely." Ivy bobbed her head without hesitation. "No one can get you here."

Josh didn't look convinced, but he was resolved to try anything that got him out of the children's home. "Okay, where do we start?"

Ivy gestured with her hand. "Come with me. I'll show you."

EVEN THOUGH IVY DIDN'T want to dwell on it, Jack's instructions for getting Josh to talk were at the forefront of her brain. Her first task was to explain to Josh what they were doing. Once he was settled with a small trowel and a bunch of pots, he seemed intrigued by the work. Enough so that he barely glanced up as he started.

"How did you learn how to do all this?" Josh asked as Ivy settled a few feet away and began transplanting plants. "I mean ... did you take a class or something?"

"Not a class." Ivy shook her head and wiped the back of her hand over her brow. It was early in the season, but the greenhouse was warm. "My father always enjoyed working with plants – my mother to a certain degree, too – so they taught me."

"Did you always know you wanted to own your own place like this?"

"No, I went through a phase where I wanted to do a lot of different things."

"Like what?"

"Well, I wanted to be a garden gnome when I was five."

Josh lifted his eyes, confused. "What?"

Ivy chuckled at his mystified expression. "It's true. My mother had this garden gnome for years and he always hung out close to the tulips and daffodils in the spring. Since those were some of my favorite flowers, I was convinced the garden gnome had my dream job."

"Didn't you know he wasn't real?"

Ivy shrugged. "I had a big imagination when I was a kid. I'm sure you were the same at that age. I thought he was real for a long time."

"But ... he's plastic." Josh's baffled expression caused Ivy to snicker. "How could you possibly think he was real?"

"I don't know. I just did. Didn't you have toys – maybe a stuffed animal or something or an action figure – that you thought were real when you were a kid?"

"No. I always knew they were fake. I didn't even like playing with toys all that much."

He was thirteen, Ivy reminded herself. He was at an age where playing with toys was considered beneath him. It happened to all kids once hormones and middle school came into play. "Well, that makes me a little sad. What did you like to play with when you were younger?"

Josh shrugged, noncommittal. "I don't know. I liked video games."

"What about your parents? What did you do with them? I mean, I know your father took you morel hunting – that's always fun – and he taught you about cars and stuff. What else did you do?"

"Not a lot. He was always busy at work."

"What about your mother?"

Josh's shoulders hopped again. "I don't like to think about her a lot. It makes me sad."

"I can imagine." Ivy's heart went out to him. "Still, you must have good memories, something that you enjoy looking back on. What did she do before she got sick?"

"She liked to run ... and work outside."

"What did she do with you?"

"She didn't do a lot with me," Josh replied, his hands dirty from packing the earth around his transplanted tomato plant. "She was always too busy for me. She said I was needy and wanted too much attention."

The boy's sharp response threw Ivy for a loop. "I'm sure she didn't mean that. She probably just said it one day because she was frazzled ... or tired ... or maybe something else went wrong."

"Maybe, but she still said it."

"Yeah, well, that's terrible." Ivy was beginning to realize that Josh was a lot more damaged than she initially realized. Not only had he watched his father die right in front of him, but he was also carrying around a lot of unhappiness revolving around his mother's death. He was trapped in a dark hole of despair, this little man, and she had no idea how to help him.

For the first time since Jack insisted they were ill-equipped to deal with his needs the previous night, Ivy truly understood what he meant. Josh needed a therapist, someone to talk to and help him work out his pain. Ivy wasn't that person, although she was still determined to help.

"So, tell me about the rest of your family," she prodded. "I know you said you didn't see them a lot before this happened, but it's important we know who is out there."

"So you know who to try to bug to take me in?"

"So we know everything there is to know about your situation and can make the best decisions going forward," Ivy clarified. "Your future is the most important thing to all of us."

"Okay." Josh let loose a long sigh. "I don't know how it will help, but I'll tell you what I know. It's a short and sad story."

Ivy managed to keep her smile in place, but just barely. "I still want to know."

"Fine. Don't say I didn't warn you."

Seven

Annette Hargrove had a baby in her arms and a toddler wrapped around her ankle when she answered the door of her Gaylord home. She looked harried ... and also a bit murderous, causing Jack to take an inadvertent step back and Brian to swallow hard.

"Um ... Mrs. Hargrove?" Brian cleared his throat to get his bearings.

Annette nodded without hesitation. "I am. If you're here selling something, though, I don't have time to buy." She moved to shut the door, but Jack quickly stopped her by inserting his foot in the space between the frame and door.

"Ma'am, we're not solicitors," Jack volunteered. "We're police officers with the Shadow Lake Police Department."

"Oh." Annette furrowed her brow, confusion evident. "I can't remember the last time we were in Shadow Lake. We don't have occasion to visit that often because there's nothing for the kids to do there. What's this about?"

"Abraham Masters."

Jack didn't miss the dark look that momentarily passed over Annette's face. It was obvious she wasn't expecting that answer.

"I have even less to do with Abraham than I do with Shadow

Lake." Annette's tone was clipped. "If he sent you over here for some reason ... well ... I don't know what to say. We haven't seen each other in more than a year and I have no intention of breaking that streak now."

Jack and Brian exchanged a quick look, something unsaid passing between them.

"Ma'am, we're here because Abraham is dead," Jack said after a beat. "He was killed in Shadow Lake yesterday and we're trying to gather information."

"Oh." The look on Annette's face didn't exactly reflect sadness. In fact, she looked more surprised than upset. "Well, come in." She stumbled a bit as she held open the door and Jack decided to help her out by scooping up the toddler and giving him a tickle around the ribs.

"And who is this?"

Annette smiled as the little boy giggled. "That's Jefferson. He's two going on thirty. He's a bit clingy today." She gestured toward the infant sucking on a pacifier in her arms. "And this is Hunter. He's teething and won't stop crying."

"It seems like you have your hands full," Brian noted as he followed the woman through the house. Even though she was clearly busy, the house was fairly neat except for the toys that were scattered about. It was clear that Jefferson liked to spread out when being rambunctious.

"I do," Annette confirmed as she sat in an armchair in the living room and automatically started rocking back and forth to keep the baby quiet. "We have an older son, too. His name is Carter and he's at school. We decided we were going to have one more, which is how we ended up with Jefferson. This little guy ... well ... he was a surprise." Even though she was clearly exhausted, she gave the baby's diapered rear end a pat and caused him to smile up at her. "Some surprises are okay."

Jack smiled at the small family, his mind momentarily drifting and causing him to wonder how many children he would have with Ivy. He doubted very much they could handle three. Two seemed like a nice number – mostly because they wouldn't be outnumbered – and there was always the chance, he told himself, they might have one and be happy with that.

"Tell me what happened with Abraham," Annette instructed, drawing Jack back to the here and now.

"He was in the woods morel hunting," Brian replied. "He was shot."

"Shot?" Annette wrinkled her forehead. "I saw that on the news. They didn't give a name or anything. I had no idea that was Abraham."

"We didn't release the name," Jack explained. "We wanted to contact next of kin, although there doesn't seem to be a lot of options. You're only one of a handful of people we found who had ties to Abraham."

"Our ties were tenuous at best," Annette volunteered. "Even when my sister was still alive, I never much cared for Abraham."

"Your sister was Melanie Masters, right?"

Annette nodded. "She was three years older than me, but we were close growing up."

"And she died about a year ago, right?" Jack pressed.

Annette's expression turned sad. "Yeah. She slipped away in the hospital. When she was first admitted, I was hopeful they would be able to find out what was wrong with her. They ran a lot of tests – a freaking lot of them – and they always came up empty. No one had any idea what was going on.

"The longer she was in the hospital, the weaker she got," she continued. "She was fading away in front of us and no one could do a thing about it. I don't even remember when I recognized the fact that she was going to die. I wasn't surprised when she did, though. I was still gutted. She was my only sister."

"It sounds like it was a horrible situation," Brian noted.

"It definitely was." Annette licked her lips and shook herself out of her reverie. "I guess I'm confused why you're here. Abraham and I were no longer family or anything. I'm not sure why you decided to inform me of his passing."

"We want to talk to you about Josh," Jack said.

"Oh." Annette pursed her lips. "I should've seen that coming. I can't believe I didn't even ask about him. He has to be a wreck. He was close with Abraham, especially toward the end when Melanie was slipping away. This must be hard on him."

"It hasn't been easy," Jack confirmed. "You see, my fiancée and her brother were in the woods morel hunting. They're the ones who stumbled across Josh and contacted us. Josh was ... confused, I guess would be the right word ... when we tried to question him yesterday."

"I don't think I'm following," Annette said. "Why would Josh be confused?"

"Things happened quickly," Brian replied. "A man with a gun approached them in the woods, Abraham told Josh to run and then it was over quickly. We believe Josh is in some sort of shock."

"Oh." Annette had an expressive face, but it was blank now. "Are you saying he's not speaking?"

"He's speaking," Jack countered. "He's very upset and admits that he couldn't hear things properly at the time – that things were muffled – but we're hoping that talking to someone he knows might make him feel more comfortable."

"Muffled?"

"That's a sign of shock," Brian explained. "Things slowed down for him. He panicked. His heart was pounding. He couldn't focus on more than one thing. It's a normal reaction in situations like this, especially when dealing with a child."

"That's too bad." Annette looked thoughtful as she bounced the baby on her lap. "As for talking to him, we were never that close."

"He's your nephew."

"Yeah, and he never liked me," Annette said. "My son Carter and Josh were about the same age. I grew up in Bellaire but moved to Midland for several years during college. That's where I met my husband and we stayed there for his work for a bit.

"When we moved back to the area, we landed in Gaylord because that's where my husband got a job," she continued. "That meant we saw Melanie about once a month. I would've liked it to be more often, but we couldn't always manage it.

"Carter and Josh were five when I returned," she said. "They knew each other from family parties and Christmas celebrations but never spent a lot of time together. Melanie and I wanted them to be close and set up play dates, but it didn't exactly work out as we planned."

"And why is that?"

"The boys didn't like each other. Josh was more of an introvert, liked books and puzzles. Carter was a boy's boy and wanted to wrestle and occasionally bite. Yeah, he was a biter. I'm not proud of it and he eventually grew out of it, but he spent a good year there biting anybody who was brave enough to touch him."

For some absurd reason, Jack had to fight the urge to smile. "I see."

"Josh wasn't a bad kid or anything, but he was quiet and introspective," Annette explained. "He simply didn't bond with people as well as he did books."

"Even his mother?"

"Oh, he loved Melanie," Annette supplied. "He went through a phase where he practically clung to her no matter what she was doing. If she was outside in her garden, he wanted to be out there, too. He seemed to need and want all of her attention."

"What about Abraham?" Jack asked, leaning back on the couch so he could rest the toddler on his lap. The boy had lost interest in playing with his watch and fallen asleep. Jack was happy to serve as a pillow as long as it kept the boy quiet. "Was Josh close with his father, too?"

"Listen, this is going to sound horrible given what happened yesterday, but I never liked Abraham," Annette volunteered. "I always thought he was a bit full of himself. He believed in traditional roles around the house, that a wife should cook and clean and the man bring home the bacon and then eat it. If you expect me to shed a tear for what happened to him, I can't do it."

Jack was taken aback. "Did you want him dead?"

"Did I want him dead?" Annette puzzled out the question. "I would've much preferred my sister live. I don't think that's what you're asking, though."

"I guess I'm confused," Jack hedged, absently running his hand over the toddler's back to keep the youngster calm. "What does one thing have to do with the other?"

"Oh, well, I'm convinced that Abraham killed Melanie," Annette answered without hesitation. "I think she didn't live up to his idea of the perfect wife and he killed her."

Brian shifted on his seat, uncomfortable and yet intrigued all the same. "My understanding is that your sister had some underlying medical condition that killed her."

"My sister was the picture of health up until she suddenly got sick two years ago," Annette corrected, shifting the baby so he could sleep with his head on her shoulder. "She was never sick a day in her life. When I got the chicken pox, so did she, only she got over it in like three days and I was down for two weeks. She was always the healthy one and she never got sick."

"They must have at least some idea what killed her," Brian prodded. "Medical mysteries aren't exactly common in this day and age. Sure, they happen, but most doctors can at least narrow things down to a heart ailment or something."

"To this day, we have no idea what killed Melanie," Annette said. "The doctor never did figure it out and the autopsy was inconclusive. She just ... stopped breathing."

"You must have a reason for believing that Abraham had something to do with her death."

"I do." Annette bobbed her head. "He was having an affair. He didn't know that I knew about it, but Melanie knew. She was going to leave him and then suddenly she got sick. She couldn't have left him after that even if she wanted to because she needed his insurance."

The story didn't make a lot of sense to Jack. "So, you're saying that Abraham was having an affair and Melanie found out about it. Right when she was going to leave him, she got sick."

"Yup."

"Did the doctors run blood panels for poison?"

"They did," Annette confirmed. "I suggested it right away."

"And they came up empty?"

"Yes. They said they couldn't find anything in her blood that suggested poison," Annette replied. "I knew, though. It had to be Abraham. He made a big show of sitting by her bedside and holding her hand. Then, every night when he left the hospital, he went to see his girlfriend."

"How do you know that?"

"I followed him several times," Annette answered, her cheeks flushed with color. "He went to a hotel and met someone. My sister was fighting for her life in the hospital and he couldn't keep it in his pants long enough to be faithful to her while she was suffering."

Jack scratched the side of his nose. "I don't blame you for being angry. However, you have no proof that your sister was poisoned."

"I feel it in my bones."

Annette was so earnest Jack couldn't argue with her. "Well, we'll ask around and see what we come up with. If Abraham had a girlfriend, that might give us a motive for murder. I don't suppose you know this woman's name, do you?"

"No. I don't know who she is. All I can say is that she looked about my sister's age and was blond."

"Well, we'll see what we can dig up." Brian rubbed the back of his neck as he internally debated how to ask the next question. Finally, he figured he had no choice but to take the bull by the horns and blurt it out. "What about Josh?"

"What about him?" Annette asked. "I thought he was okay."

"He's alive, but he's very far from okay," Jack replied. "He's a traumatized boy who spent the night after witnessing his father's murder in a group."

"That's awful." Annette's features twisted. "You're going to ask me to take him, aren't you?"

Jack could practically feel the trepidation rolling off the woman. "He's your nephew. If you don't take him, I am afraid what will happen. He could become a ward of the state. We're going to check with a few other relatives, but there aren't a lot of you guys out there."

"I can feel you judging me," Annette said, her eyes filling with tears. "I don't blame you. He's my sister's only child and I should want to take him. I don't, though. I have more than I can handle already.

"I love my children, don't get me wrong, but they're a lot of work," she continued. "We were planning on two with a wide gap between them so we could give them both a lot of attention. We had a big birth control fail, and our plans flew out the window.

"I'm emotionally wrecked right now," she continued. "I don't get more than a few hours' sleep a night and I'm exhausted. I don't have anything to give Josh.

"Still, if I thought he would end up someplace awful, I would obviously step in," she said. "Josh needs a lot of attention, though. He's a needy kid. The way he attached himself to my sister troubled me on a lot of levels."

Jack pictured the way Josh bonded with Ivy, the way he clung to her even though he barely knew her. "I can see that. He's still your nephew."

"He is," Annette agreed. "He's my nephew and my sister would want what's best for him. I think having access to psychologists and people who know how to help him through his grief is what's best for him.

"I haven't seen him since Melanie's funeral," she continued. "He didn't even look at me that day. He's never liked me. We never bonded. We're just ... not close. I have to focus on my own children. I know that sounds harsh, but they're my priority.

"I feel bad for Josh," she continued. "He's always been a lost and lonely kid. I blame Abraham for isolating him because he only wanted Josh to hang around with the right kinds of kids. You know, the kids who had a mother at home instead of working. Abraham set ridiculous rules and it made Josh think a certain way.

"Do you know, he once told me I was a bad mother because I worked part-time at the library?" she said, incredulous. "Josh said that. It wasn't Abraham. Josh learned how to parrot everything his father said."

"That's terrible and I don't agree with it," Jack said solemnly. "We're still in a bad place here. Josh has no one. If we can't find a family member to take him in, he'll become a ward of the state."

"And maybe that's best for him," Annette persisted. "They'll be able to give him the counseling he deserves, and he'll have people who focus solely on him for a time, which is what he desperately needs.

"I have three children of my own," she continued. "I can't give them the attention they need. How am I supposed to focus on Josh without neglecting my own children? Or, switch it around, how am I supposed to focus on my own children and ignore Josh? Someone would end up hurt in the equation and I don't want anyone getting hurt."

Jack bit back a sigh. He wanted to press the woman further – he was legitimately worried what would happen to Josh, and how that would affect Ivy because she was already attached to the boy – but he also knew she was speaking the truth. It was obviously hard for her, she was a good person, but she recognized her limitations. She simply could not give Josh what he needed.

Brian clearly felt the same way because he slowly got to his feet. "Thank you for your time. We'll ask around about what you mentioned, your sister's illness and all, and see what we can come up with."

"We'll keep in touch," Jack added, carefully transferring the sleeping toddler to the playpen next to the couch. The boy didn't as much as move a finger at the change in location.

"I really am sorry." Annette was sincere as she walked them to the front door. "I feel awful and it's probably something I'll always carry around. I can't take him, though. I'm barely hanging on here."

Jack was sympathetic to her plight and patted her shoulder. "I think you're doing admirably well here. As for Josh, we'll figure something out. If you want to see him down the line, I'm sure that can be arranged."

"Yeah. I'll talk to my husband when he gets home tonight. The least we can do is visit."

"I'm sure he'll like that," Jack said.

"Actually, I'm betting he won't like it," Annette countered. "I still want to see him. He's all I have left of Melanie, after all."

"Here's my card." Jack handed a small piece of cardboard to her. "If you have questions later, or something occurs to you, don't hesitate to give me a ring. My cell phone is on there, too. I'll be in touch when I know more."

"Thank you." Annette held open the door as they filed out. "I hope you find who did this."

"Oh, we'll find who did this. We won't let a murderer get away with a brutal killing like this in our town. I promise you that. We will find answers. It simply might take some time."

Eight

Ivy took a break from Josh long enough to touch base with her father.

"How are things going out here? Have you been keeping up with the list I left?"

Michael lifted his eyes, amused at his only daughter's bossy nature. She planted her hands on her hips as she watched him work, an air of authority wafting off of her. "Things are fine."

"Do you need help?"

"Not last time I checked."

"But ... it's kind of busy."

Michael tilted his head to the side as he regarded his offspring. Ivy was always the higher maintenance of his two children. Max had better self-esteem and a healthy ego as a youngster. Ivy took time to grow into her ego, although it was fairly impressive now that she was an adult. "Everything is fine out here, Ivy," Michael said after a beat. "Is something wrong in there?" He indicated the greenhouse with a head bob.

"No." Ivy shifted from one foot to the other. "He's fine."

Something about the way she said it alerted Michael that she was struggling with something she didn't want to admit to. "What is it, kid?" Michael searched Ivy's face for a clue. "What has you so upset?"

"Nothing has me upset. Why do you think something has me upset?"

She sounded too defensive for comfort. "Because you're out here instead of in there bonding with your young acolyte," Michael replied calmly. "Did he say something to upset you?"

In truth, Josh said several things to upset Ivy. She was working overtime not to dwell on them, though. "He's a sad kid," she said finally. "A lot has gone wrong in his life. He's a little upset about it. Can you blame him? I mean ... he saw his father shot and killed in front of him."

"I don't blame him for being upset about that." Michael was matter of fact. "I think you're worried his anger might be a bit more than you can deal with, though."

Ivy couldn't shutter her surprise quickly enough. "What makes you say that?"

"Because I know you, daughter." Michael winked at Ivy. "I can tell when you're worried. You don't hide your emotions very well. Everything you feel is right on the surface."

Ivy had no idea if that was supposed to be a compliment or a dig, so she let it slide. "He's very angry. You're right about that."

"You can't fix that, Ivy." Michael took a pragmatic approach. "At least not right now. Josh needs to work through a few things and you can't be the one to fix everything for him. It's not your job."

"I want to help him."

"That's because you have a giving soul. This is still out of your wheelhouse."

"You sound like Jack," Ivy grumbled. "He said pretty much the same thing to me."

"Well, Jack is a smart man." Michael's lips curved at Ivy's scowl. "He snapped you up, didn't he?"

Ivy shot her father a withering eye roll. "Ha, ha."

"I mean it."

"Whatever." Ivy pressed the heel of her hand to her forehead. "I just came out for a quick breather. I was hoping you would order lunch and have it delivered. I have money in my purse, which is under the cash register."

"I'll order lunch. Is there anything Josh doesn't like?"

"I asked. He said a burger with ketchup and pickles is fine. Maybe some fries, too."

"I'll get on it."

"Thanks." Ivy flashed a brief smile before turning on her heel to return to the greenhouse. Michael stopped her by calling out.

"Hey, Ivy?"

"What?"

"You're doing the best you can," Michael noted. "I think you're practically perfect but, if I did have a complaint, it would be that you take things to heart too much. There's no reason to do that now."

Ivy stared at him for a long beat. "I think it's too late for that. I feel responsible for him."

Michael heaved out a sigh. "I figured as much. Still, you can only do what you can do."

"I'm going to do the very best that I can for him. There is no other option."

"I know." Michael offered a half salute. "I'll order lunch and bring it to you guys in a little bit. Will you be okay until then?"

"I'll be fine." Ivy brushed off her father's concern. "I'm just complaining about nothing. I do that sometimes."

Michael watched her go, conflicted. While it was true Ivy liked to randomly whine and she got a kick out of fighting with Jack over certain things, she wasn't a rampant complainer. He couldn't help but worry over his daughter. For the life of him, though, he had no idea how to make things better.

TAMMY VICKERS-MASTERS lived in a senior assisted living facility on the highway between Shadow Lake and Bellaire. While not a blood relative of Abraham Masters, she was one of the few people in the area who had any ties to the man. She seemed surprised when Brian and Jack stopped in to inform her of Abraham's death.

"That's terrible." Tammy shook her head as she sat on the small loveseat in her private room. "I was never close with Abraham or anything, but I'm sorry to hear something happened to him. I'm kind of shocked, if you want to know the truth. I had no idea when I saw that story on the news that it was Abraham who passed."

"What was your relationship with Abraham, ma'am?" Brian asked, his smile amiable as he sat in a chair across the way. He gave the appearance of being relaxed, but he often felt out of sorts when he had to visit facilities like this. They made him uncomfortable.

"We didn't have much of a relationship," Tammy admitted. "I married his father when Abraham was in his thirties. He was always nice and polite to me – a gentleman, so to speak – but it's hardly as if we bonded."

"You knew him after he married Melanie, right?" Jack asked. "You got to see them together."

"I did." Tammy narrowed her eyes. "What is this about?"

"Your stepson was killed in the woods," Brian replied. "He was murdered. We're trying to find a culprit. To do that, we kind of need to find a motive."

"Ah. I understand." Tammy said the words, but Jack wasn't sure if she meant them. "Well, I don't know what to tell you. We saw Abraham and Melanie together on holidays and special occasions. Abraham spent a decent amount of time with his father, even after he got sick and had to be put in a home, but I didn't know him very well."

"We're looking for observations," Jack noted. "Did you ever observe any problems between Abraham and Melanie?"

"What kind of problems?"

Jack shrugged. "I don't know. Any kind you can come up with."

"See, I think you're fishing for something specific, but you don't want to say because you would rather I volunteer the information," Tammy noted. "You want to know about the rumors that Abraham was cheating on Melanie, don't you?"

"Are you aware of those rumors?"

Tammy bobbed her snowy head. "You've been talking to Melanie's sister, haven't you?"

"We've talked to a few people," Jack hedged. "We really can't get into too much detail over that."

"Don't worry. I know how the sister felt about Abraham. She was convinced that he was having an affair even as Melanie lay dying in the hospital."

Her derisive tone told Jack that Tammy believed something else. "You don't think so?"

"I don't think Abraham was a particularly good husband," she clarified. "He was a bit full of himself and had antiquated ideals when it comes to what a woman should be doing in the home. I found some of the nonsense he spouted to be insufferable.

"Don't get me wrong, if a woman wants to stay home and take care of a house and children, I think she has that right," she continued. "I don't think anyone else should force that decision on her, though."

"I happen to agree with you," Jack offered. "Please continue."

"Despite his faults – and Abraham had a number of them – he wasn't a terrible man," Tammy explained. "When Melanie got sick, he was a wreck. He spent almost all his free time with her. He still had to work to keep the insurance, and he made sure he did his job, but he was with Melanie every chance he got."

"What about a hotel room?" Brian queried. "We heard that Abraham was meeting someone in a hotel room at night."

Tammy snorted. "Now I know you've been talking to the sister. She ran that story on me, too."

"Were you at the hospital when Melanie died?" Jack asked. "The way you make it sound, you only spent time with Abraham's father and didn't have a lot to do with the family after the fact. I thought your husband died a few years before Melanie got sick."

"He did," Tammy confirmed, bobbing her head. "I was still living on the outside when Melanie got sick. My incarceration here is more of a recent thing." Her smile was rueful. "When I heard about Melanie, I went to the hospital. I wanted to help if I could. I understood Abraham had a lot going on and wanted to sit with Melanie if he needed it, maybe even keep an eye on Josh or something."

"Were you close with Josh?"

"No." Tammy took on a far-off expression. "I don't think that boy was close with a lot of people. He always seemed nervous and jumpy when I saw him, as if he was expecting something bad to happen at any moment."

"Something bad *did* happen," Jack pointed out. "His mother died."

"She did and that's a terrible thing," Tammy agreed. "Josh wasn't exactly broken up about it when it happened. He seemed more ... numb, I guess would be the word ... than anything else."

"I think that's a fairly normal reaction, especially for a boy that age," Brian noted. "Boys have a harder time expressing themselves than girls."

"I'm not finding fault with Josh," Tammy said. "I don't want you to think that. I always thought he was a weird kid, though. I believed that Josh would've been better, maybe a little less clingy, if his parents had tried again to give him a little brother or sister. After the death of Jenny, they basically didn't try again."

Jack furrowed his brow, confused. "Jenny? Who is that?"

"Josh's sister."

"Josh doesn't have a sister," Jack argued. "In fact, when I asked him about it last night, he said he was an only child."

"Technically he doesn't have a *living* sister," Tammy explained. "He had a baby sister for a brief time, though. She didn't live long."

"And what happened to her?" Brian asked, his heart already aching because he understood he was going to hear something awful.

"SIDS. That Sudden Infant Death Syndrome thing. She was fine when Melanie put her down for the night but cold and gone when they woke the next morning. It was a tragedy that shook everyone."

Brian and Jack exchanged a weighted look. This was the first they were hearing about this sad tale.

"How old was Josh when the new baby was born?" Brian asked after a moment's contemplation.

"Um, I think he was about ten." Tammy screwed up her face in concentration as she did the math in her head. "Yeah, that sounds right. He was almost eleven when she was born, but not quite. His birthday that year was right around the time of the baby's death. I remember Melanie struggling to put together a small family party because she was so upset about Jenny."

"I can't even imagine how difficult that was," Jack said. "If I'm grasping the timeline correctly, that would've happened about a year before Melanie got sick, right?"

"Basically," Tammy confirmed. "I think Jenny's death changed Melanie forever. She was never the same after. Heck, Abraham wasn't either. Melanie, though, almost seemed resigned to death when it was getting near. She seemed to think she had it coming for not waking up and realizing something was wrong with Jenny so she could save her."

"That's not how SIDS works," Brian pointed out. "There's often no rhyme or reason when it happens."

"I know. That's what I tried telling Melanie at the time. She was inconsolable. Right before she died, she told me she was at peace with what was to come because that meant she would be reunited with Jenny. That's all she seemed to care about."

"What about Josh?" Jack queried. "Wasn't she sad about leaving him?"

"Of course. She was a good mother, even if things didn't go how she expected the last year of her life. She knew Josh would be okay with Abraham, though. They were tight and she knew Abraham would take care of him."

"The only problem is that Abraham is gone now, too," Brian noted. "We're trying to find a family member to take Josh, provide a stable home for him, and we're not having a lot of luck. We were hoping you might be able to come up with some names for us."

"I can try. I'm not sure how much good I can do for you, though."

"If you can give us anything, we would greatly appreciate it."

"Let's see what I got."

IT WAS ALMOST THREE when Ivy looked at the clock and realized she was running out of time. She promised Dana she would have Josh back to the group home before four, which meant they needed to get moving.

"Okay. I think that's enough for today." Ivy clapped her hands together to dislodge the dirt and removed the protective apron she wore to keep her clothes clean before hanging it on a hook near the greenhouse door. "We need to get you cleaned up so I can drive you back to the home."

Instead of reacting with happiness – or even resigned agreement – Josh made a face that was right out of the Teenager's Guide to Being a Pain in the Posterior Handbook. "I don't want to go back to the home." Josh remained focused on the tomato plant he was staking. "I want to keep doing this."

"I told you gardening was cathartic." Ivy beamed at the boy. "We can do more of it if Dana allows you to come back for a visit. For now, though, I promised I would drive you back in plenty of time for dinner and it's getting late."

"I don't want to go back."

Ivy managed to keep her smile in place, but just barely. Josh's moody nature – the way he swung between anger and happiness at the drop of a hat – was starting to wear on her. She understood about grieving, acknowledged Josh was going through the worst thing imaginable, but she couldn't quite wrap her head around his bursts of anger and petulance. "You have to go back. You can't stay here. The only reason Dana even allowed the visit is because I promised to get you back at a reasonable time."

Josh lifted his chin, his green eyes defiant. "Call and tell her I'm staying here. I want to stay with you. I hate that place."

"I understand that." Ivy chose her words carefully. "I don't blame you for being unhappy there. I have no choice but to take you back. You know that. We talked about this."

"Well ... I changed my mind."

"You're not allowed to change your mind."

"I did, though." Josh's demeanor was cool. "I don't want to go back there. I want you to make it so I can stay here. I know you want to keep me close to you so ... make it happen."

Ivy blinked several times in rapid succession. Josh's belligerent attitude throwing her for a loop. Finally, she found her voice. "Josh, if I try to keep you, the police will be called. They'll take you from my house and I won't even be able to visit you again. I'll be barred from the home and you'll be disallowed to visit me. Is that what you want?"

"No."

"Then why are you pushing this?"

Josh's lower lip trembled, reminding Ivy he was a child in pain. His little bursts of pouty behavior weren't on purpose. The boy was trying to come to grips with his father's death. This was after his mother's long illness and death. How much was one person supposed to take without falling apart?

"Don't cry." Ivy moved closer and patted his shoulder. "We're going to figure all of this out. I promise. I don't have a choice in taking you back, though. If I don't, we're both going to end up in trouble and get absolutely nothing out of it."

Josh lifted his tear-streaked face so he could meet Ivy's steady gaze. "You would keep me if you could, right?"

Ivy nodded without hesitation. "Absolutely. I can't, though. I have to take you back. I don't want to give Dana a reason to keep you from visiting. I'm guessing you don't want that either."

"Definitely not." Josh swiped at his tears. "I guess we should be going then."

Ivy smiled as she extended her hand. "Yup. There's no rule we can't stop for ice cream on the way back. I only said I would get you back in time for dinner. I didn't mention anything about not ruining your appetite for that dinner."

Josh broke into a wide grin. "That sounds like a plan."

Nine

Jack and Brian stopped at the children's home long enough to touch base with Dana. Since she was Josh's caseworker, they were expected to have regular conversations regarding his mental state and attitude. She didn't seem surprised when they let themselves into her office after a single knock and motioned them in while making a brief notation in a file.

"I'm surprised you guys didn't stop by earlier," Dana admitted. "I thought you would be here first thing in the morning."

"We spent the day trying to track down relatives for Josh," Brian explained. "If you're wondering, it didn't go well. He has an aunt, but she's already overloaded with three kids of her own."

"She won't take him?" Dana's expression was hard to read. "Does she know he'll likely become a ward of the state if she doesn't?"

"We explained things to her."

"Well, we can't force her." Dana was pragmatic as she flipped shut the file folder. "It's probably best we know now. We don't want her taking Josh if she's not going to treat him well."

"I don't think she's a bad person," Jack cautioned. "She was simply already overwhelmed."

"And she probably knows what's best for her lifestyle," Dana noted.

"I'll start sending out inquiries for foster homes and see what I come up with."

"That's probably best," Brian agreed, leaning back in his chair. "What can you tell us about him otherwise?"

"I can tell you that he doesn't want to be here. He's extremely unhappy and views this place as a cage. I can't say I blame him."

"Is that why you let him go with Ivy?" Jack was legitimately curious. "I didn't think that was normal operating procedure where you guys are concerned."

"I let him go with Ivy because she wasn't going to take no for an answer and he actually opened up and talked to her," Dana replied. "He wasn't going to talk to anyone else so I took a shot."

"Is he back?"

"No, but Ivy texted to tell me she's on her way," Dana answered. "She didn't go into a lot of specifics about their afternoon, before you ask, but said things were fine. I can press her when she gets here."

"I'll handle the pressing," Jack said, making a face when Brian smothered a chuckle under his hand. "Not that kind of pressing. You have a filthy mind."

"With you two I can never tell," Brian said. "As for Josh's little excursion with Ivy, I don't see how it could cause problems. She's good with him. More importantly, she's responsible."

"She has pink hair," Dana reminded him, causing Jack to bristle.

"There's nothing wrong with her hair," Jack snapped. "She's a good person. In fact, you should thank your lucky stars she agreed to come here and help you today."

Instead of being offended, Dana was amused. "Slow your roll, Romeo," she teased. "I was joking. There's no reason to get worked up."

"He doesn't have much of a sense of humor where Ivy is concerned," Brian explained. "He thinks she walks on water."

"I do not." Jack rubbed his forehead. "What I think is that she doesn't deserve the crap you two are saying about her."

"Oh, he really is smitten," Dana teased, grinning. "He's kind of cute, huh?"

"Sadly, they're both cute," Brian said, returning the smile for a beat before sobering. "As for Josh, I don't know what to tell you. We still don't know who did this and have no idea where to place him. I'm not sure how much help we're going to be."

Dana was the sort of woman who was used to rolling with the punches. "You can only do what you can do. We'll figure it out."

"I hope so," Jack said, his eyes flicking to the glass panel in the door when he saw Ivy walk by with Josh at her side. She was laughing and smiling, but he knew that wouldn't last when he told her about his day. "We'll be in touch when we have more information."

"I'll move ahead with what I have," Dana said. "We'll find the right placement for Josh. It's simply going to take a little bit of time to figure out exactly where that is."

IVY WASN'T IN THE MOOD to cook so when Jack suggested they stop by the Shadow Lake diner for dinner she jumped at the chance to let someone else handle food preparations.

"You look tired," Jack noted as he slid into the booth across from her. "Was it a long day?"

"It felt like a long day," Ivy conceded, resting her chin on her hand as she sighed. "I thought I was helping, but I'm not sure, in the end, if that's true."

"What do you mean?"

Ivy shrugged but told Jack about her day, starting from the beginning and wrapping up with Josh's reticence to return to the home. She was beyond frustrated with the system even though she knew the individual people involved were working overtime to make things happen. "He was depressed when I dropped him off. He barely said a word."

"Honey, you can't take that to heart." Jack rested his hand on top of Ivy's and stared into her sea-blue eyes. "That kid has been on one endless rollercoaster for his entire life it seems. His father died yesterday. He's not going to get over that in twenty-four hours."

Ivy balked. "I know that. I'm not an idiot. I know he's not going to get over it right away. He was enjoying himself before I told him it was time to return to the children's home. He was opening up."

"What did he say?"

"He told me a few things, like how his mother didn't want to spend a lot of time with him and how he felt neglected to the point where he was still angry when she died. I think part of the problem is that he's mad at her and himself because he thinks he should cut her a break given what happened."

"Well, I don't want to condone neglect, but I'm not sure that Josh's story makes any sense."

Ivy was offended on Josh's behalf. "He wouldn't make that up."

"I didn't say I thought he was making it up," Jack cautioned. "I simply don't believe he understands what his mother was going through."

"Nothing excuses neglect."

"Unless it wasn't neglect," Jack countered. "What if it was something else?"

"Like what?"

"Grief."

Ivy stilled, confused. "I don't understand."

Jack related his conversation with the aunt and step-grandmother, leaving nothing out. He saw no reason to keep information from her, especially since she was already knee-deep in the investigation and had no intention of backing off.

"So, from what Tammy told me, I don't think it was that Melanie was neglecting him," Jack said, wrapping up the story. "I think it was that she was wiped out emotionally from the loss of the baby and she had trouble slapping herself back together again. Tammy said it was like Melanie wanted to go at the end because she wanted to see the baby."

"That is awful." Ivy was truly horrified by the tale. "I can't believe one family was expected to go through all that without getting a break. I mean ... what are the odds?"

"I can't answer that." Jack squeezed her hand as he leaned back in his seat. "I don't know why some people are inundated with pain and others aren't. There's no rhyme or reason to it."

"Do you think some people are cursed?" Ivy asked.

Jack's lips curved. "No. I don't think some people are cursed."

"I used to." Ivy rubbed the back of her neck with her free hand as she shifted on her seat. "When I was a kid and crying all the time because the other kids didn't like me, I thought I was cursed. I knew I was different. I recognized that and so did the other kids. They didn't like those who didn't conform so they attacked whenever they could."

Jack's stomach rolled at the admission. He'd heard parts of this story before, and he didn't like how sad it made her. "Honey ... ."

Ivy held up her hand to cut him off. "No. This isn't a 'poor Ivy' conversation," she said hurriedly. "I'm simply explaining that I used to think certain people were cursed. I thought maybe you did, too, because of what happened in Detroit."

Jack studied her features for a beat. "You mean when I was shot and left for dead by my former partner?"

Ivy nodded. "Don't you think that makes you cursed?"

"No." Jack smirked as she furrowed her brow. "At the time, I thought that was the worst thing that could ever happen to me. Now I'm grateful it happened."

Ivy was understandably dubious. "You're grateful that you almost died? I don't understand."

"If I hadn't been shot that day, if I hadn't spent weeks feeling sorry for myself and insisted on leaving the city, I never would've come here and met you." Jack's eyes sparkled as he snagged Ivy's gaze. "Do I want to be shot and go through that again? Absolutely not. Would I if it meant keeping you forever? Oh, honey, without a doubt. You're the best thing that ever happened to me."

Ivy's cheeks burned, a mixture of pleasure and embarrassment washing over her. "That was possibly the sweetest thing anyone has ever said to me."

"I meant it." Jack was earnest. "I can't be cursed because I have you. It's that simple."

Ivy stared at him for a long beat and then broke out into a wide smile. "Do you have any idea how lucky you're going to get tonight?"

Jack chuckled at her enthusiastic reaction. "No. If you want to tell me, though, I'm all ears."

"Oh, you just wait." Ivy bobbed her head knowingly. "I'm going to show you exactly how non-cursed we both are as soon as we get out of here."

"That sounds like the best offer I've had all day."

JACK AND IVY WERE A mass of sweaty hands, hammering hearts and fervent kisses when they hit the cottage. Jack barely managed to remember to check the front door to make sure it latched properly behind them before dragging Ivy toward the bedroom.

They weren't married yet, but Jack absolutely loved practicing for the honeymoon.

Once they were finished, Jack rolled Ivy so she was on top of him, her chin resting on his chest as he absently ran his fingers up and down her spine.

"We're definitely not cursed," Ivy murmured as she brushed a kiss against Jack's chest. "In fact, that was the exact opposite of being cursed."

"I thought so, too." Jack pressed a kiss to her forehead. "Oh, honey, you have no idea how much I love you." He clutched her close as he stretched, marveling at the way her body fit against his. "If we spent every moment of the rest of our lives like this, I would die the happiest man in the world."

Ivy let loose a throaty chuckle. "You're easy to satisfy."

"It's not that. It's simply that you're everything I've ever wanted so you don't have to struggle to satisfy me."

"I think there was a compliment buried in there."

"Me, too." Jack's eyes were half shut when he glanced at the nightstand, frowning when he saw the light glowing on Ivy's phone. "Someone must have called. I didn't hear your cell go off earlier, did you?"

"No, but I turned it to silent on the ride back from town." Her eyes were mischievous. "I didn't want to risk an interruption."

"That's probably wise. I would've definitely thought we were cursed if we got interrupted."

Ivy giggled, the sound warming Jack to the soles of his feet. "That's exactly why I turned it to silent." She grunted as she leaned over to grab the phone. "I wonder who bothered calling."

"If it's Max, I'm going to thump him next time I see him."

"It's probably my mother."

"If I thought your father couldn't take me, I might thump her, too."

Ivy laughed as she touched the voicemail button and pressed the phone to her ear. "Wow. I have three missed messages. I wonder how that happened."

Jack grew concerned as he tipped his chin down and watched Ivy listen to her voicemail. Leaving three messages was the mark of a desperate person. He couldn't help but wonder if something bad had happened to one of Ivy's family members.

As it turned out, it was so much worse.

"It's Josh," Ivy said after a beat.

"What does he want?" Jack asked.

"He's upset and wants me to come get him. He hates the home."

"Honey, you can't." Jack stared hard into her eyes. "You know you can't do that, right?"

"I know." Ivy tamped down her agitation at Jack's worried look. "I'm not an idiot."

"You're definitely not an idiot," Jack agreed. "In fact, you're the smartest person I know."

"I don't feel smart." Ivy pressed a button on her phone and went to the next message. "Oh, geez."

Jack knew who it was before he even had to ask the obvious question. "Josh?"

Ivy nodded. "He's crying and says that he won't be able to sleep if I don't come get him. He's afraid he's going to have nightmares."

"Ivy, look at me." Jack's tone was stern enough that Ivy had no choice but glance up. "I love that you have a huge heart and want to help, but there's nothing you can do for that kid tonight." Jack was firm. "I know that he's upset because life has thrown him nothing but hand grenades for thirteen years straight, but you can't fix this for him."

"You act as if I don't know that," Ivy barked, her temper coming out to play. "I know that I can't fix this. I didn't say I could fix this. Why do you assume I'm going to run out of the house in an attempt to fix this?"

"Because I've met you." Jack refused to back down. "You can't help yourself. You want to be a hero."

"That's rich coming from you," Ivy muttered under her breath as she switched to the third message. To absolutely no one's surprise, Josh was at it again. This time he was so hysterical Jack could hear him through the phone because Ivy was forced to hold it away from her ear.

"Let me listen." Jack took the phone from her and pressed it to his ear, wrinkling his nose when he heard the harried boy beg Ivy to drop whatever she was doing so she could pick him up. He suggested that he might die of a broken heart if she didn't. Even though Jack knew the boy was simply trying to better his own situation, he couldn't stop himself from being upset at the emotional manipulation.

"Geez. He really knows how to lay it on thick, huh?"

Ivy's expression was unreadable as she propped herself on one elbow and licked her lips. She didn't immediately answer.

"Honey, will you tell me what you're feeling?" Jack asked after a beat. "I mean ... I think I know ... but I would like to be sure."

"I'm feeling guilty," Ivy supplied.

"You can't go to him. The home is locked down for the night. There's literally nothing you can do."

"That's not why I feel guilty."

Jack knit his eyebrows. "What do you mean?"

"I feel guilty because I don't want to get him," Ivy admitted, averting her eyes. "I feel guilty because I'm relieved that I don't have to go to him. I want to help, you know I do, but it occurred to me today that he needs more than I can give."

"I believe I told you that already."

"Really?" Ivy drawled, rolling her eyes. "Do you want to pull out an 'I told you so' now?"

"I see what you're saying and I take it back." Jack softly rubbed at the tension building in the base of her neck. There was nothing Ivy liked more than a good massage. He was hopeful he would be able to lull her to sleep now with his magic hands. "You're wise and beautiful."

"Ha, ha." Ivy rolled her eyes. "He's so desperate and needy that I don't know what to do for him. No, seriously. I don't know if anyone has enough to give him. I think it's because he's lost so much that he can never get back. He has a hole inside that can't be filled."

"You have a way with words and I think you're probably right," Jack said. "I don't know how to make this better right now, though. I know we'll figure this out, but I don't even know where to look to start things off."

"I have faith that busy mind of yours will come up with something." Ivy rested her head back against his chest. "Until then, I thought maybe we could dream walk tonight. We haven't done it in almost two weeks and I'm worried we're both so restless we won't sleep unless we agree to go on a trip together."

Jack and Ivy's minds joined before they even started dating. Somehow Jack drew her into his dreams, something that didn't freak her out and caused her to want to stay despite the dark corners of his mind. The dream walking had turned into an adventure of sorts, but one they didn't want to abuse.

"I think a shared dream is just what the doctor ordered tonight," Jack noted. "How does a white sand beach and ocean breeze sound to you?"

"Great. Don't forget the hammock."

"Oh, I could never forget the hammock." Jack gave her a soft kiss before returning her phone to the nightstand. "It's going to be okay. We'll come up with a plan that allows everyone to get what they need. I promise."

"I know. I have faith."

"Good. Now ... I suggest you dress yourself in a coconut bra for this dream. I have very specific ideas."

Ivy giggled. "Lead the way."

"Oh, I intend to. Brace yourself; it's going to be a hot and sandy ride."

Ten

Jack woke first and immediately smiled when he heard Ivy lightly snoring beside him. She insisted she didn't snore and he was determined to record her as proof. He managed to snag his cell phone from the nightstand but didn't get a chance to turn it on before noticing her bare feet poking out from the end of the covers. On a whim, he leaned over so he could touch her foot and wasn't surprised to find it ice cold.

"What are you doing?" Ivy murmured, her eyes remaining closed.

"I don't understand why you do this." His plan to record her snoring ruined, Jack abandoned his phone and focused on Ivy's freezing feet. "Why must you poke your feet out from under the covers? How is that even remotely comfortable?"

Ivy shrugged, noncommittal. "I don't know. I don't like my feet being hot."

"It drives me crazy." Jack pressed a kiss to the bottom of her foot and caused her to squirm. "I was going to record you snoring, by the way, but I became distracted by your feet."

"I don't snore."

"Oh, you snore."

"I do not."

Jack opened his mouth to push the issue and then thought better about it. "Fine. You don't snore." He gave her foot another kiss before propping himself up on an elbow to study her face. "You look well rested," he said finally. "I was worried you wouldn't sleep because of the messages from Josh."

"I slept."

"Did you sleep *well*, though?"

Ivy sighed. She was used to Jack hovering when he thought he had something to be concerned about. "I slept fine, Jack."

"I can't help it if I worry, honey." Jack refused to back down. "That's what happens when you love someone."

Ivy didn't bother to stifle her sigh as she rolled flat on her back and stared into his eyes. "We talked about this. You don't have to worry about me. Do I feel guilty about not being able to help him more than I already have? Yes. That doesn't mean I don't understand that I've done all I can do."

Jack wanted to believe her. From his perspective, the problem with that was Ivy often acted before she thought about the consequences. "What do you plan to do today?"

Ivy knew exactly where he was going with the question but refused to react out of anger. "I thought I would spend the day sitting on the couch and thanking my lucky stars that I have you in my life."

Jack scowled. "There's no reason to get testy."

"I'm not being testy. I plan to write a list of all the things I love about you. That will take all day and keep me out of trouble."

"And here we go," Jack muttered as he rolled to his knees and stared directly into her eyes. "I don't want to fight."

"You always want to fight." Ivy knew she sounded like a petulant teenager but she didn't care. "That's what keeps your skin young and fresh."

Despite himself, Jack barked out a laugh. "I think you like to fight as much as I do. That's not necessarily a bad thing when you like to make up, too. As for this stuff with Josh ... well ... I know you're trying to be as careful as possible. I get it. However, I would be lying if I said I wasn't worried about your heart getting broken in this matter."

Ivy struggled to a sitting position and shifted her body so she was forehead to forehead with Jack. "I know I can't fix this for him." She kept her voice low and even. "I can't stop myself from wanting to help him, but I'm not an idiot. I know what you're really worried about."

Jack carefully slid a strand of her morning mussed hair behind her ear. "What am I really worried about?"

"That I'll blame myself when he's moved to a new home," Ivy replied without hesitation. "That I'll take it upon myself when he falls apart because he can't see me any longer. I'm not an idiot, I know that he will have an adjustment period at a new home and they'll want me to take a step back."

"They will," Jack confirmed. "The thing is, honey, I love that you're so giving and want to help, but I'm worried that you're getting too attached to him and he's becoming too reliant on you. It's not going to be good for him to be dragged away from you again. I worry how he'll react."

Ivy thought about the voicemails the previous night. "Yeah. I'm worried, too."

"So, what are you going to do with your day?" Jack was keen to hear her answer. "Are you going to check on him?"

"I'm going to call him," Ivy replied after a bit of thought. "I don't want him to think I suddenly lost interest in him. That doesn't seem fair. It will crush his ego."

"Okay. I don't think a call is the end of the world."

"Then I'm going to go morel hunting with Max," Ivy added. "Our previous trip ended early and I still want to bring home one big score for a few recipes I like."

Jack made a face. "Are you going to make me eat these recipes?"

"Probably."

"Ugh. You know I hate the morels because they taste like feet."

"You just spent five minutes kissing the bottoms of my feet," Ivy pointed out. "I would think that means you secretly like feet."

Jack stared at her for a long beat, caught between annoyance and adoration. "I like your feet," he clarified finally. "I like the way you wiggle when I kiss your feet."

"I think you've got a fetish."

"That's still not how you're going to get me to eat those mushrooms," Jack noted, firm. "You're going to have to offer me something special to even get me close to those mushrooms."

Ivy giggled. "Like what?"

"Like ... a moonlit walk to the lake one of these nights when it gets warmer," Jack replied. "I want it to be a really hot night, for the record, and I'm going to demand all of your attention when it happens."

"When don't you have all of my attention?"

"During morel season."

Ivy snorted, genuinely amused. "I can see you've given this some thought. While a moonlit walk sounds romantic, I'm guessing there's more to the request."

"There's definitely more to the request," Jack confirmed. "Once we're down at the lake, I want to go skinny-dipping."

Whatever she was expecting, that wasn't it. Ivy was agog at the suggestion. "Wow. You just had that one ready, didn't you?"

Jack shrugged, noncommittal. "I haven't been skinny-dipping since I was a teenager and that was in a retention pond at a nearby apartment complex. It left a little something to be desired."

"I've never been skinny-dipping."

Jack jerked up his head at the admission. "What? How can that be? You grew up with that lake right behind your house. It's within walking distance."

"So?" Ivy was mildly uncomfortable with Jack's stare and fought the urge to squirm. "I never skinny-dipped before. Get over it."

"Oh, this is awesome." Jack's enthusiasm threw Ivy for a loop. "Are you really telling me that your first skinny-dipping experience is going to be with me? I think that's the best thing I've heard all day."

Ivy's lips curved down. "Why do you say that?"

"Because I like sharing first experiences with you and I plan to be the only guy you ever skinny-dip with. That's ever ... because we're getting married. I will be the only one."

"Yes, but how is that fair for me?" Ivy challenged. "You've skinny-dipped with other women. It's not the same for me."

"I *did* skinny-dip," Jack conceded, his smile turning rueful. "I did not have a woman with me when it happened."

"But you said ... ."

"I said that I hadn't skinny-dipped since high school and I did it in a retention pond," Jack clarified. "I didn't say I was with someone. For the record, I tried to talk my girlfriend at the time into doing it, but she didn't like the idea. She thought the water was dirty."

"So ... you went by yourself?"

"It was hot."

Ivy pressed her lips together to keep from laughing at Jack's response.

"Go ahead and giggle." Jack poked her side. "At the time I thought I had the worst luck. Now I think it was a sign from God."

"That you're not cursed?"

"Maybe." Jack ran his hand over her hair to smooth it. "I like the idea that it's something we can do together and that neither of us have ever shared the experience with anyone else."

"You're kind of schmaltzy sometimes. Has anyone ever told you that?"

"Nope. I don't care either." Jack pressed a soft kiss to the corner of her mouth. "Now I can't wait for it to get warm enough for us to do this. A couple weeks, right?"

"At least June." Ivy couldn't help but smile at his enthusiasm.

"Either way, I'm looking forward to it." Jack gave her another kiss. "In fact, I'm so looking forward to it I'll even eat your feet mushrooms tonight. I don't care how gritty they taste."

"Oh, wow. The power of true love," Ivy teased.

Jack grabbed her around the waist and wrestled her to the mattress as Ivy giggled. "And don't you forget it. How about I give you a little preview? We'll pretend we're skinny-dipping in the shower."

"I've had worse offers."

JACK AND BRIAN'S FIRST stop of the day was to talk to Dr. Wayne Jordan. He served as Melanie Masters' doctor toward the end of her life and there were enough questions surrounding Melanie's ailment that the two police officers believed it bore further investigation.

If Jordan was surprised by the request, he didn't show it. Instead he ushered the two men into his office and poured coffee before settling down to business.

"I guess I'm not sure what you expect from this conversation," Jordan hedged. "Mrs. Masters has a right to medical privacy even in death."

"I understand that," Brian said, leaning back in his chair. "The thing is, we've got a murder and we can't quite wrap our heads around motive. We understand you never came up with a cause of death for Melanie Masters."

"That's not entirely true," Jordan hedged. "We knew her cardiovascular system was under duress. While we don't have a definitive reason, her heart simply stopped working the correct way and we couldn't fix the problem."

"Mostly because you had no idea what the problem was, right?" Brian queried.

Jordan ran his tongue over his teeth as he debated how to answer. Jack could practically read the agitation rolling off the man's shoulders.

"We're not trying to blame you for this," Jack interjected, taking Jordan by surprise. "We don't think you were remiss or somehow missed something. We're trying to understand what happened."

"We certainly don't blame you," Brian agreed. "Abraham Masters was shot and killed on our turf. We can't seem to find a motive. His son has been left an orphan and all this happened a year after Melanie Masters died under mysterious circumstances. We're simply trying to figure out what's going on here."

Jordan relaxed, although only marginally. "I understand you're dealing with a difficult situation. I heard the story about the shooting two days ago. I didn't even realize that it was Mr. Masters until someone mentioned it last night. Did he survive the injury for more than a few minutes?"

"No." Jack shook his head, understanding what the doctor was asking. "He didn't suffer. There was no saving him. He died quickly."

"That's too bad." Jordan rubbed the back of his neck as he shifted in his chair. "I'm not sure what I can tell you."

"We're looking for observations," Brian said. "We know it's not scientific and we're not asking you to testify in court. Still, we've heard a few things. How would you describe Abraham's relationship with his wife?"

"He seemed to dote on her to some degree," Jordan replied without hesitation. "He was engaged with her medical care, asked the appropriate questions, and sat with her when she was feeling poorly."

"That's it?"

Jordan held his hands palms out and shrugged. "What else was he supposed to do? This was not a situation where he could jump into the thick of things and serve as her doctor. We worked hard to come up with a diagnosis. We honestly believed we could save her if we simply discovered what was causing her symptoms."

"Did you ever narrow it down?" Jack asked.

"I don't know." Jordan took on a far-off look as he flicked his eyes to the window next to his desk. "It bothered me more than I want to admit that we couldn't find a cause. We checked her heart and lungs. We ran endless tests, to the point where her insurance provider was giving us grief about the cost of the tests."

"That seems ... cruel," Brian muttered.

"I don't know that I would use that word, but it was annoying," Jordan said. "That didn't stop us from running the tests. We were convinced that we would find an answer and save her."

"Obviously that didn't happen."

"No. She was sick but stable for a long time and she was perking up a bit," Jordan explained. "She wasn't exactly what I would call strong, but she wasn't weak either. We were going to upgrade her and start a series of flushes for her system when she crashed again. This time she was sicker than ever and we knew we wouldn't be able to bring her back. She was simply too weak."

Jack rubbed his forehead as he considered the statement. "And you don't know what caused her to crash?"

"No. We have no idea. One minute we were telling her husband and son that she was getting better and the next we were desperately trying to keep her from slipping away. It was the oddest thing."

Brian cleared his throat, his discomfort obvious. "Did you ever consider that she might have been poisoned?"

Jordan didn't so much as blink at the question. "Of course. We ran all the standard panels. We came up empty. Something was killing her but, if it was poison, it was something we didn't know to test for."

"Well, that answers that question." Brian slid his eyes to Jack. "I thought maybe if the affair rumors were true that there was a possibility that Abraham was poisoning her to get her out of the way."

"You heard rumors that Mr. Masters was having an affair?" Jordan asked, furrowing his brow. "May I ask where those rumors came from?"

"Melanie Masters' sister," Brian answered. "She seems convinced her brother-in-law was running around on her sister."

"She's not the only one who believed that," Jordan said. "A couple of the nurses swear they saw him with a woman in the parking lot. Who that woman is, I can't say. They didn't recognize her.

"As for how Mr. Masters was with his wife, he seemed to genuinely love her," he continued. "I know that some people are good actors and whatnot, but he seemed to be devoted to her and I could tell the fact that she was so ill was ripping him apart."

"What about Josh?" Jack asked. "How was he with his mother?"

"Needy," Jordan answered immediately. "He seemed intent on keeping his mother's focus on him. He didn't want to leave at night, insisted on being close to her. It seemed he was unnaturally attached to her."

"Or that he worried someone was going to hurt her," Jack mused. "Maybe he wanted to stay close because he thought his father was poisoning her."

"Why wouldn't he say something if that were true?" Jordan challenged.

"Because, if he thought it was his father, his loyalties were probably stretched," Brian offered. "My guess is Josh had his suspicions, which is why he wanted to stick so close to his mother. He definitely knows more about what happened to his father than he's letting on."

"Do you think he talked someone into killing his father?" Jack asked, his mind working overtime as he ran the scenario through his head. "Josh might have loved his father, but if he blamed him for his mother's death, there's a possibility that he somehow talked someone into stepping in and doing something."

"How could a kid do that, though?" Brian challenged. "I mean ...

he's a kid. No matter how upset he is, I can't see an adult taking up his cause without some sort of proof. And, if he had proof, why not give it to the police? I simply don't understand."

"I'm not sure Josh understands what he's feeling," Jack noted. "He's gone through a lot. We need to figure out if Abraham was really having an affair. That would give him motive to kill his wife."

"But how would he kill her without setting off the poison panels?" Brian asked.

"Oh, that's not as hard as you think," Jordan answered for Jack. "Certain things are caustic and they don't show up on our standard panels. We ran several specialized panels, too. I'll double check again so I can refresh myself on her levels, but I don't believe anything stood out."

"Well, we need to figure it out." Brian was firm. "I want to make sure that boy isn't a target. That means we need a motive for Abraham Masters' murder. Cheating on his dying wife seems as likely a motive as anything else."

"Then we should get on it." Jack pushed himself to a standing position and smiled at Jordan. "Thank you for your time. We might be in touch again."

"I will go through Melanie's records this afternoon," Jordan promised. "I'll see if I can find something that sticks out. I was fond of her. She was a nice woman. If I can help you solve the mystery of what happened to her, I'm more than willing to put in the time."

"Thanks for that. We might need those answers before this is all said and done."

Eleven

Max found Ivy rummaging through her purse when he let himself into the cottage shortly after ten. He expected her to meet him on the front porch – they were both excited to get some morel hunting in – but she barely looked up when she heard the door open.

"If you expect to win the competition by looking in your purse, you're going to be sucking my dust all day," Max teased.

"What?" Ivy lifted her eyes and frowned. "Oh, no. I'm just trying to figure out what happened to the money I had in here yesterday."

"It's missing?"

"It seems to be." Ivy thoughtfully tapped her bottom lip. "I told Dad to get money out of my wallet for lunch at the nursery yesterday, though. Maybe he forgot to put the money back when he was done."

"That doesn't sound like Dad," Max argued. "In fact, I'm surprised he even took your money at all. He usually likes to be the provider."

"Yeah. I had Josh, too. Maybe he didn't have enough to cover all of us."

"Maybe." Max remained unconvinced. "Do you want me to call him?"

"No." Ivy shook her head. "I'll see him at the nursery later. I'll just ask him then. It's not a big deal. It was only fifty bucks. I'll just run to the ATM when we're finished."

"You mean when I'm finished wiping the floor with you," Max corrected, causing Ivy's eyes to narrow.

"Oh, you know what?" Ivy got to her feet and left her purse on the dining room table. "Bring it on. I'm going to make you cry when I'm finished with you."

Max snorted. "Oh, puh-leez. I'm going to beat the pants off you ... although not in a yucky way because you're my sister and I just realized that came off grosser than I thought it would."

"Yeah, yeah." Ivy rolled her eyes and snagged the pillowcase from the counter. "Are you ready to watch me win?"

"I'm ready to watch you whine."

"Then let's do it. We don't have all day. Some of us have work to do."

Max snickered. "I work harder than you do five days a week ... and twice on Sunday."

"You don't work weekends."

"You know what I mean."

"I do," Ivy confirmed, bobbing her head. "I know that you're an exaggerator of the highest order. It's never more apparent than when you say you're a better morel hunter than me."

"Oh, you're going down."

"I guess we'll just have to see about that."

BRIAN AND JACK LET themselves into the Masters' house with the key Abraham had on his body at the time of his death. The house itself was a nondescript ranch. It matched all the other houses on the street and was eerily quiet when they entered.

"What are we even looking for here?" Jack asked as he moved into the living room, frowning at how clean and sterile the house felt.

"I don't know that we're looking for anything," Brian replied. "We have to start somewhere, though."

"I guess." Jack wandered over to look at the mantel above the fireplace. It was filled with framed photographs and Melanie Masters was the central figure in all of them. "Do you think Abraham put all these up to appease Josh?"

"I don't know." Brian knit his eyebrows as he stared at the photographs. "It does seem like a bit of overkill, doesn't it?"

"By a longshot. Here's one of her and the baby, though." Jack pointed. "It looks as if she was in the hospital."

"There's another one down here with her and the baby," Brian noted, moving closer to the photo so he could study the image. "This one is here in the living room. She looks happy."

"She looks happy in all the photos. I'm guessing she was a happy person."

"Until she realized she was going to die."

"Yeah, well, I'm betting that wouldn't make anyone happy." Jack gave the photo in front of Brian another long glance before frowning and turning back to stare at the living room. "You know, I think Abraham Masters was something of a neat freak."

"What makes you say that?" Brian was genuinely interested as he surveyed the room with fresh eyes. "I guess everything in here has a place, huh?"

"It doesn't look like a home."

"I don't know what you mean by that. It's clearly a home. Abraham and Josh shared it together."

"I know that," Jack countered. "It's just ... look at the cottage. Ivy and I both live there, but it feels ... different. It's never neat. Er, well, I guess it's neat when Ivy knows we're going to have company. There's always something that's never put away, though."

"Are you saying that Ivy is a slob?"

Jack scowled. "No. I'm saying that we live in that house together, so it feels differently than this house. I mean ... this place is sterile. In our house, Ivy kicks off her shoes by the front door and sometimes they end up under the couch.

"That evil cat of hers leaves hair all over the place and occasionally rips all the toilet paper off the roll and drags it through the house when he feels she's not paying enough attention to him," he continued. "There are magazines on the table, lotion-making stuff on the counter, and right now there are two pillowcases just hanging around in case she gets a yen to go morel hunting."

"Oh, I get what you're saying." Brian's eyes lit with interest. "You're basically inferring that there's no life to this house."

"It doesn't feel as if anyone lives here," Jack confirmed. "What did the sister say? She said Abraham had certain ideas for how a wife was supposed to take care of a household. Apparently he kept that up himself after her death."

"Maybe the photos are a way to pretend he was mourning harder than he really was," Brian suggested. "I mean ... they are overkill. Maybe we should check the rest of the house."

"Yeah." Jack rubbed the back of his neck, contemplative. "Let's check Josh's room, too. Maybe if there's something in there that looks as if he might want it we can take it to him at the home."

"That sounds like a plan."

"Then, when we're done with that, we'll question the neighbors," Jack added. "They might be able to give us some insight into Abraham and what he's been doing since Melanie's death."

"That sounds like an even better plan. Let's get to it."

IVY AND MAX WERE content to search for morels in comfortable silence for the bulk of the afternoon. They only had about thirty minutes left before they had to call it a day and head to work – and the competition was still fast and furious – when Max decided to call his sister on her melancholy mood.

"What's wrong with you?"

The question caught Ivy off guard. "Nothing is wrong with me. I'm winning."

Max made an exaggerated face. "You're not winning. Keep dreaming. Something is definitely wrong with you, though. You seem lost in your own head."

"Oh, well, I guess I am." Ivy heaved out a sigh. "Jack thinks I'm getting too involved with Josh. He's worried. After what happened last night, I think he might have a point."

Max swooped down to grab a cluster of morels, making sure to avoid two of the offerings as he sorted through his haul. "Be careful. There are false morels over here." Even though he desperately wanted to win, Max also wanted to make sure his distracted sister didn't pick dangerous mushrooms. "What do you think Jack has a point about?"

"The fact that Josh is a very needy child and I can't give him what he so clearly desires."

"Which is?"

"A mother."

Max stilled, confused. "A mother? You think he wants you to be his mother? That seems a bit ... out there ... to me."

"I don't think he wants me to be his mother," Ivy clarified. "It's more that he thinks of me as a motherly figure. I don't like it either because I'm young and hot. I'm definitely not old enough to have a thirteen-year-old child."

Max chuckled, legitimately amused. "Good point."

"He's alone." Ivy sobered. "He has no one. Jack told me his aunt won't take him."

"How come?"

"She's got three kids of her own. Jack says she's overwhelmed and barely holding on with her own brood."

"I guess I can understand that."

"I *want* to understand that, but I'm still agitated by it," Ivy admitted. "I mean, if something happened to you, do you think I would let anyone else take your kid when I could keep a piece of you close?"

"Oh, that's kind of cute." Max tweaked the end of Ivy's nose with his dirty fingers, grinning at the way she growled. "I love knowing that you would swoop in and take Max, Jr. That makes you a good sister."

"It's not about being a good sister."

"Oh, but it is." Max was firm. "You fancy yourself the best sister in the world."

"I am."

"I know. I'm the best brother, too." Max's grin was impish as he snagged Ivy's gaze. "I also know that if something happened to me you would move heaven and earth to make sure that any offspring I produce would be happy. That's who you are."

"You need to find a steady girlfriend before you focus on offspring," Ivy muttered.

"And I have time." Max patted the top of her head, delighted when she rolled her eyes. "You're going to be the one procreating before me. You and Jack are pretty much ready to add to our small but awesome family."

"We're not having kids right away," Ivy argued. "We want to spend at least a year together before we add kids."

Max's eyebrows flew up his forehead. "You've already talked about it?"

"We have."

"Wow. You guys are such good grown-ups." Max danced away when Ivy attempted to playfully swat him. "As for the rest, I get what you're saying. If something happened to you and Jack, I would make sure that I had your kids and that they were well taken care of. Not all siblings are created equal, though."

"Meaning?"

"Meaning that maybe Melanie and her sister weren't as close as we are."

"Sometimes I think we're too close," Ivy said. "On the flip side, I get what you're saying. We have a unique relationship. Not everyone can mirror that relationship. You're basically saying that I'm being judgmental."

"Basically," Max agreed. "Still, I get why you're worried. I feel responsible for Josh, too. In fact, since you're taking a step back but obviously still worried, I'm going to head over to the home when I'm done here."

Ivy couldn't hide her surprise. "You are?"

"I am."

"Is this because you want to hit on Dana?"

"I forgot Dana even worked there, but I'm totally going to hit on Dana when I see her." Max's eyes twinkled. "I'm also going to see if I can get Josh to hang out with me at the lumberyard for the afternoon. That will get him out of the home but make it so he's not fixating on you. I think it's a solid solution to your problem."

Ivy didn't want to admit it, but she liked the idea a great deal. "If you have the time, well, that would be great."

"Your enthusiasm is overwhelming."

"I'll also make you a cherry pie," Ivy offered. "I was going to make Jack blueberry anyway. There's no reason I can't make two pies."

"Now that's what I'm talking about." Max glanced at his watch and then shook his head. "We have fifteen minutes and we're basically tied. We'd better start moving if we expect to fill these bags."

Ivy mock-saluted. "Yes, sir." Her expression softened when she saw Max's eyes gleam with wicked intent. "Also ... thanks for doing this. I know it's not how you planned to spend your day."

"It's okay." Max gave Ivy's hand a small squeeze. "I feel responsible for him, too. If we hadn't been in the woods that day, I shudder to think what would've happened to him. He could've gotten lost."

"Or hunted," Ivy added. "A lot of terrible things happened to him."

"We'll make sure nothing else terrible happens to him," Max promised. "We can work together on this. It doesn't all have to fall on your shoulders."

"You really are a good brother," Ivy offered. "It's kind of annoying sometimes."

"I know. Why do you think I do it?"

"Because you want to be the best at everything."

"Good point."

GILLIAN DORCHESTER STOOD on her front porch and suspiciously looked Brian and Jack up and down. They'd flashed their badges upon knocking – and explained why they were there – but Gillian remained skeptical of their intent.

"I'm not buying any of those policeman's ball tickets you guys are always hawking."

Brian flashed a genuine smile even though he knew the woman was going to be a righteous pain in the behind. She had a certain "air" about her, and it was one Brian recognized from time spent with his mother-in-law. For the record, at least in Brian's head, that wasn't a good thing.

"We're not selling anything," Brian said, keeping his voice calm and even. "We're just looking for information."

"I haven't done anything," Gillian fired back. "If you expect to search my house, you need a warrant. I know my rights."

"We don't want to search your house." Now that she brought it up, Brian was mildly curious if she was keeping something illegal in the house. Ultimately it didn't matter. Bellaire was not their jurisdiction. "We're trying to find out information about Abraham Masters."

"Oh." Gillian was mollified, although only slightly. "I heard what happened to him. That's a terrible thing."

"It's definitely a terrible thing," Brian agreed. "We're trying to figure out who would have motive to kill him. One of the things we heard is that he was having an affair and we were wondering if you would happen to know who he was seeing."

"An affair, huh?" Gillian tilted her head to the side, her eyes nothing but brown slits. "Who told you he was having an affair?"

"We heard it from multiple people," Brian lied. "What we haven't heard is a name so we can confirm it."

"Do you think this woman is responsible for killing him?"

"Do I think she pulled the trigger herself? No. Do I think that someone might've been angry about the affair, enough to kill Abraham? Yes."

"Yeah, I wanted to kill him a bit myself when I found out," Gillian admitted, shifting from one foot to the other. "I really liked Melanie. She was quiet and kept her yard looking good. She didn't drop in all the time for coffee or to chat. She basically kept to herself."

"And that makes her a good neighbor?" Jack asked.

"Absolutely." Gillian bobbed her head. "For the record, I liked Abraham, too. He wasn't loud or obnoxious. I wasn't happy he was having an affair when his wife was so sick, but I didn't figure it was any of my business."

"How did you know he was having an affair?" Brian queried. "Did he tell you?"

"No, I saw him with his little ... um, friend ... a few times," Gillian replied. "Melanie was in the hospital for weeks over that final stay.

Abraham's woman stopped by here at least three times when Melanie was in the hospital. I thought it was disgusting."

"Do you happen to know her name?" Jack asked, hopeful. They were finally getting somewhere. If they could track down the mistress, they might finally get some answers.

"I didn't recognize her myself but, when I pointed her out to Patty Lancaster down the way, she knew exactly who I was talking about," Gillian answered. "She's a local woman. Apparently she and Abraham went to high school together."

"That's very interesting," Brian noted. "What's her name?"

"Ellen Woodbridge. She lives on the other side of town."

"Have you seen her in recent weeks?"

"No, but I haven't been paying as much attention," Gillian admitted. "Melanie isn't around for Abraham to cheat on any longer. He's a widower, not a philanderer. I don't care who he wants to romance now. I cared back then because Melanie cared."

"Did she ever mention the affair to you?" Jack asked.

"No, but I'm pretty sure she knew about it. I saw her crying once after she got in an argument with Abraham. He left her on the porch and took off. She seemed so sad and alone that day I couldn't help but feel for her."

"Well, thank you for your time." Brian flicked his eyes to Jack. "Let's go see Ellen Woodbridge. I've got a few questions for her."

"I think we both have questions."

Twelve

Ellen Woodbridge was a pretty woman. She was in her late thirties but still looked as if she was in her twenties, and she had a soft and welcoming smile. It faltered a bit when Brian held up his badge and asked if they could talk to her.

"This is about Abraham, isn't it?" Ellen looked resigned.

"It is," Brian confirmed.

"I knew you would come." Ellen held open the door to usher Jack and Brian inside her small and homey Cape Cod house. She forced a tight smile as she led them down the hallway and toward the kitchen. "I'm making fresh banana bread. I also have a pot of tea out. I don't have coffee. Sorry. You'll have to make do with the tea."

"The tea is fine," Brian replied, exchanging a quick look with Jack. He knew his partner was thinking the same thing he was. Ellen Woodbridge was about to be a fountain of information. They could put up with tea if it meant they got that information.

"I happen to love tea," Jack announced as he selected a chair at Ellen's round dining table. "My fiancée prefers tea as well. She has coffee in the house for me, but I've become used to the tea. I even like it now."

"I simply don't like the taste of coffee," Ellen offered. "It tastes bitter to me."

"I think it's an acquired taste," Brian said as he got comfortable at the table.

"Yes, well, here you go." Ellen delivered three cups of steaming tea to the table before sitting and fixing Brian and Jack with a weighted look. "You want to know about my relationship with Abraham, don't you?"

"Why do you assume that?" Brian asked.

"Because I saw the news yesterday. Abraham was killed in a freak accident in Shadow Lake. You're trying to decide if it was murder and when going through Abraham's history you stumbled across me."

"That's not entirely true," Jack hedged. "We know that Mr. Masters wasn't killed in a freak accident. It *was* murder."

Ellen stilled, her features going deathly white. "Are you sure?"

"We're sure," Brian confirmed. "There's no doubt Mr. Masters was specifically targeted for death. What we're trying to work out is if it was pre-meditated and someone followed him into the woods with the express purpose of killing him or if it was a crime of opportunity."

"Meaning that someone stumbled across him and decided to kill him in that moment," Ellen surmised. "Wow. I can't believe he was actually murdered."

"He was." Brian leaned back in his chair and regarded the attractive woman with keen interest. "You don't seem all that shook up."

"Is that how I'm supposed to react?" Ellen queried. "Did you think I would burst into tears and drop to my knees? Not every female shows emotion by turning into a soap opera character."

Jack furrowed his brow as he picked up on the bitterness of her tone. "I'm guessing things didn't end well between you and Abraham."

"They didn't, but I wasn't angry enough to kill him, if that's what you're worried about."

"We don't yet know what we're worried about," Brian supplied. "What we need from you is a rundown of your relationship with Abraham. We need to know how you hooked up and when it ended."

"And if I don't feel comfortable giving that information?"

Brian stared at her for a long beat. "Then we'll have to get a warrant to compel you," he said finally. "That's not the way we want to go about things, but we need to know who Abraham might have ticked off enough to come after him. Your potential involvement in this is not something we can gloss over."

"Right." Ellen blew out a sigh. "I figured as much. You have to understand, I'm not exactly proud of what happened. It was never my intention to be the other woman."

"We're not here to judge you," Jack offered. "We simply need to know the nature of your relationship."

"Well, I think you're going to be disappointed, but here goes." Ellen took a bracing breath and then launched into her tale. "Abraham and I knew each other from high school. We both lived in town and, much like Shadow Lake, the class sizes weren't overly large. Everybody knew everybody.

"Abraham and I first hooked up sophomore year and we were together until graduation," she continued. "It was a nice relationship, full of very little drama, but it wasn't exactly passionate or anything. He was simply there and made things easy for me.

"I went to college in Traverse City and he went to Michigan State University," she said. "The distance was too great and we broke up about a month into our college separation. I honestly thought that was it. I never expected us to get married or anything. It wasn't even a consideration.

"By the time Abraham returned to Bellaire he was engaged to Melanie," she supplied. "I heard about him being back in town before I saw him. I didn't think much of it before I ran into them at the grocery store. They seemed ... fine. I didn't get a passionate vibe from them either. I remember thinking at the time that it was entirely possible that Abraham wasn't a passionate guy."

"That changed at some point," Jack prodded. "When?"

"I'm not sure exactly when things shifted," Ellen replied. "I know that when Josh was ten Abraham enrolled him in a special program at the park. We had a day camp of sorts and it involved sports, outdoor activities, and arts and crafts stuff. You know the drill."

Brian nodded without hesitation. "We have something similar in Shadow Lake."

"I'm a teacher," Ellen explained. "That means I have summers off. I take on temporary work at the day camp to enhance my income."

"And that's how you came into contact with Abraham again?" Jack queried.

Ellen bobbed her head. "Basically. We saw each other from afar here and there over the years, don't get me wrong. Mostly it was at the grocery store or theater or something, so we just waved at each other and went on our merry way. Once I started seeing Abraham on a regular basis, there was a subtle shift.

"Nothing happened that first year ... or even the second year Josh was at summer camp, for that matter," she continued. "We talked when we saw each other, maybe flirted a bit. It was harmless flirting, though. We made eyes at each other and laughed at lame jokes, but it was nothing serious."

"When did it turn serious?"

"Well, this is going to sound awful, but it happened right after the baby died," Ellen replied. "Jenny. When I first heard Melanie was having a baby I was angry, although I had no right to feel that way. At that point Abraham and I were simply talking and having the occasional cup of coffee."

"You knew you wanted more, though, didn't you?" Brian asked.

"I did. I felt a spark with Abraham that had never been there before. I felt as if I'd missed something the first time and wanted to see what that something was now that I had a second chance."

"Did he feel the same way?" Jack was legitimately curious. "I mean ... he had a new baby at home. Sure, the baby died, but you said the relationship didn't happen until after Jenny passed away. To me, that indicates he still had a spark burning with his wife, too."

Ellen let loose a weary sigh and rubbed the space between her eyebrows. "No matter how I explain things, I'm going to come off as the bad guy. I understand that. I'm not saying what I'm about to tell you is rational."

Brian bobbed his head. "Fair enough."

"I was convinced that Melanie purposely got pregnant to trap Abraham and force him to stay in the marriage," Ellen explained. "I thought she recognized somehow that Abraham was pulling away because he realized he'd rather be with me. Since Josh was older, I thought there was a very good chance Abraham would leave Melanie."

"That never happened, though," Jack said. "How come?"

"Because Jenny died." Ellen looked morose as she rubbed her forehead. "The baby died and Melanie was a wreck. Abraham wasn't much better off, although his grief took a different turn and that's when we started sleeping together. Like ... two days after."

"You actually started having sex right after his daughter died?" Jack was horrified.

"There's nothing you can say that I don't already think about myself," Ellen offered. "I didn't think it at the time. I painted myself as a victim back then. I think about it now, though, and I know what I did was terrible."

"We're not here to focus on that." Brian waved off Ellen's bitterness. "We want to know what happened after that."

"After that, well, Melanie got sick," Ellen replied. "At first it was just the occasional stomach ailment. You know, the flu or food poisoning. Maybe a nervous reaction to all the stress she was under. It kept going on, to the point where I thought Melanie knew Abraham was trying to sneak off and see me. Then she got really sick."

"And you kept up the affair?" Jack tried to keep the judgment out of his voice, but it was difficult.

"I don't even know if you would call it an affair at that point," Ellen countered. "We were meeting twice a week but there was rarely anything romantic happening between us. I managed to be bitter about that, but I was smart enough not to push Abraham because I knew it wouldn't end well for me.

"You see, even though I believed that Abraham loved me and wanted to be free of Melanie, I also knew Abraham would never leave her while she was sick," she continued. "Melanie needed his insurance and her ailment was getting progressively worse. At some point I came to the realization that she wasn't faking it and there was something honestly wrong with her."

"Did your relationship continue until after Melanie died?" Jack asked.

"No." Ellen shook her head, firm. "Melanie was extremely sick when it ended. Abraham was spending all his time at work and the hospital. He was ... completely detached from me."

"How did that make you feel?" Brian asked.

"Hurt and a bit foolish." Ellen let loose a dry chuckle as she clutched her hands around her mug. "By that point I think I knew it was over, but I wasn't quite ready to let him go. When Abraham called to ask me to meet him at his house – he needed to change after work and didn't have a lot of time – I thought he was going to apologize for neglecting me and promise that we would spend more time together."

"Instead he broke up with you, didn't he?" Jack understood where the story was going. "He dumped you."

"He did," Ellen agreed. "Although it didn't happen quite like you're imagining. I think it would've gone that way, mind you, but something happened that interrupted our final meeting."

Brian leaned forward, officially intrigued. "And what was that?"

"Josh." Ellen's eyes glazed with tears at the lone word. "He came home from school and surprised us. I was trying to cozy up to Abraham at the time and he was distracted from what he had to tell me and what was going on with Melanie. Josh entered the house without us knowing and found us in the bedroom."

"And how did he take things?" Jack asked. "I'm going to guess it didn't go over well."

"No. Not well at all." Embarrassment colored Ellen's cheeks. "He was at an age where he grasped why I was there right away. No one was naked or anything, it could have been perfectly harmless ... even though it really wasn't. Josh was furious, and he started screaming at his father. I mean ... real 'I hate you and wish you would die' stuff."

"I think that would be a normal kid's reaction to seeing something like that."

Ellen bobbed her head. "I do, too. I wasn't angry or anything, simply embarrassed."

"How did Abraham react to that?"

"He was calm, as if he was expecting it. He apologized to me. Said he wished we would've met in a different lifetime. Then he showed me to the door and focused all his attention on Josh. I think he kept his focus on Josh the entire time after that."

"You guys didn't see each other at all after that?" Brian was understandably dubious. "You never once tracked him down after Melanie's death to see if you could rekindle the flame?"

"No." Ellen shook her head. "I was furious the day it happened. I felt sorry for myself a few weeks after that. Then I heard through the grapevine that Melanie died and I started feeling guilty. Once I let the guilt in, it got a foothold and I realized what a shrew I'd become. I wasn't exactly proud of myself."

"Still, to have a relationship like that and never speak of it again," Jack pressed. "That doesn't seem normal to me."

"Well, I don't know what to tell you." Ellen turned rueful. "Sometimes truth is stranger than fiction. Abraham walked away from me and I let him. He focused on Josh and I fixated on trying to make myself a better person. It's a work in progress."

"Did you see him at all after that?" Brian asked.

"Not really. I saw him at the grocery store or around town. This time I did not wave. I felt like too much of an idiot to do it."

"And what about Abraham?" Jack asked. "You spent a lot of time with him for more than a year. You were talking about very serious things. Did he ever mention anyone having a grudge against him?"

"Not that I know of."

"What about Melanie?" Brian questioned. "Did she find out about the affair? Could she have told someone about it?"

"And what?" Ellen furrowed her brow. "A year after her death someone decided to take revenge for an affair that Abraham ended before his wife died? That doesn't make a lot of sense to me."

"Revenge often doesn't make sense. I need to know if Melanie was aware of the affair."

"Not that I know of." Ellen turned sad. "I don't think Melanie knew. Abraham didn't want that. For her to hurt even more after everything that happened was too much for him to bear. As for the rest, I have no idea who would want to go after Abraham. He was a good man who made a mistake. He was a bit set in his ways but that's hardly the worst thing I've ever heard."

"No," Jack agreed. "Still, though, is there anyone in your life who would want to get revenge on Abraham for ending the affair with you?"

"Not that I can think of. I'm sorry."

"Well, that's disappointing." Jack flicked his eyes to Brian. "Now what?"

His partner shrugged. "I honestly have no idea."

IVY WAS IN A RELATIVELY good mood when she cut her way through the nursery shortly before two. She'd won the morel-hunting contest (although Max was demanding a rematch) and her brother had gone out of his way to ease her emotional burden by taking Josh for the afternoon. It did Ivy's heart good to know Josh was being taken care of, getting the attention he deserved, and she wasn't mistakenly spending too much time with the young boy during his all-important grieving process.

Ivy was in such a good mood she almost missed the look on her father's face when she approached him at the checkout station. His back was to her, his shoulders hunched, and he wasn't nearly as animated as he normally was when dealing with the customers.

"How are things?" Ivy asked, poking her head into his station. "Did I mention I beat Max this morning, by the way? I picked a lot more mushrooms than he did. He didn't cry or anything, but I think he wanted to."

Michael's expression reflected panic when he swiveled to face his daughter, causing Ivy to instantly sober.

"What's wrong?" Panic licked at Ivy's heart as she struggled to read her father's expression. "What happened? Something happened, didn't it?"

Michael nodded, his shoulders stiff. "There was an accident at the lumberyard."

Ivy's heart lurched. "Josh? Did something happen to Josh?"

"No." Michael shook his head as he struggled to maintain control of his emotions. "It appears a group of logs wasn't tied correctly – or the straps broke, I'm not sure – and your brother was injured when they fell."

The momentary relief Ivy felt only seconds before evaporated. "Max? Is he okay?"

"He's at the hospital." Michael choked out the words. "That was your mother. The paramedics contacted her first. He was unconscious after the incident and he's being worked on now."

"But ... he's going to be okay."

Michael felt helpless as he held his palms out and shrugged. "They don't know yet. We have to get to the hospital."

Ivy snapped to attention. "Then let's go. What are we wasting time for when Max needs us? Let's get out of here."

Thirteen

Ivy had to practically run to keep up with her father's long strides when they hit the hospital. It was more of an urgent care facility than an actual hospital, but the Morgans were regular visitors – sometimes even customers, thanks to Ivy's penchant for trouble – and they knew their way around the building. The woman at the intake desk recognized them right away.

"Hey, Emma, how is Max?" Michael asked, doing his best to sound calm even though his heart pounded incessantly.

Since she knew how close the family was, Emma Howard took pity on him. "I don't know yet. He was unconscious when they brought him in. He's still undergoing an examination."

"Has he woken up at all?" Ivy asked, her stomach twisting when Emma shook her head. "He hasn't opened his eyes even once?"

"He hasn't been here long, Ivy," Emma cautioned. "You guys are only five minutes behind him. It's going to take a bit of time to give him a good examination."

Inherently, Ivy knew that. Her heart ached all the same. "Right. I know."

"You guys should sit down," Emma suggested, sympathy practically rolling off her in waves. "I'll give you news the minute I hear it."

"Okay." Ivy wanted to argue further, push the woman until she told her what she wanted to hear. She knew that was a wasted effort. After all, it wasn't Emma's fault that Max had been hurt. "We'll be right over here." Ivy indicated the chairs and couches in the small waiting room. "Don't forget us."

"I won't forget you."

Ivy was barely in her chair before she dug in her pocket and retrieved her cell phone. Her hands shook as she punched in Jack's number. He picked up on the second ring.

"Hello, honey. Do you miss me or something?"

Even though Ivy understood there was no way for Jack to know what happened to Max, she was irritated all the same by his jovial attitude. "There's been an accident."

Jack sobered instantly. "Are you okay?"

"I wasn't in the accident."

"Tell me what happened."

Ivy felt numb, almost disconnected from her life. She desperately wanted Jack with her to soothe the fear coursing through her veins, but she was having trouble explaining what happened because the words seemed somehow elusive.

As if reading her mind, Michael plucked the phone from her hand and pressed it to his ear. "It's Michael."

"What happened?" Jack asked, fear evident in his voice. "Is she okay?"

"She is ... in a mood," Michael replied, choosing his words carefully. "She's afraid and upset. I am, too. I simply handle it better than her."

"I still don't know what happened," Jack reminded him.

"It's Max. There was some sort of incident at the lumberyard. We're still not sure what happened. My understanding is that a group of logs that were tied together somehow got separated and Max was knocked down because of it. He has a head injury."

"Oh, geez."

Michael could practically picture Jack pinching the bridge of his nose over the phone. A year before, the man had been nothing but a random curiosity in their lives thanks to Ivy's interest in him. Now he was part of the family even though he'd yet to officially marry into it. Michael was thankful for Jack's calm presence, his huge and accessible heart, especially on days like today.

"You should probably come," Michael prodded, sparing a glance for Ivy, who was fixated on the door that led to the back of the hospital. "I know you're busy with work but ... she needs you."

"I'm already on my way," Jack promised. "There's nothing in the world that could keep me from her at a time like this. You don't have to worry about that."

Unsurprisingly, Michael already knew that. "Luna is on her way, too. Right now, Ivy and I are simply sitting in the waiting room and hoping for news."

"I'm about fifteen minutes out," Jack volunteered. "We're coming from Bellaire and there's construction. I'll be there as soon as I can."

"I know you will. Drive safely. The last thing we want is you getting in an accident."

"Don't worry about that. I'm on my way." Jack paused before hanging up. "As for Max, he has a really hard head. I know that because Ivy does, too, and they've got that in common. I have faith he'll be okay."

"I hope so." Michael forced a smile even though Jack couldn't see it. "He's a pain in the butt sometimes, but I love him all the same."

"We all do," Jack said. "I'll be there soon. Tell Ivy ... tell her what you think she needs to hear."

"She needs to hear Max is going to be okay. Until then, there's no consoling her."

"I'll give it my best shot in fifteen minutes. I promise."

MAX'S WORKERS SHOWED up several minutes later, concerned looks on all their faces. They had Josh with them, the young man's face completely ashen as he searched the urgent care lobby for a familiar face. He broke out in a wide smile when he saw Ivy.

"Hi. I wasn't sure you would be here."

Even though she was completely fixated on hearing word about

Max, Ivy internally chided herself for forgetting that Josh was with her brother when the accident happened. She hadn't even asked about him, which felt ridiculous in hindsight.

"Hey." Ivy forced a smile as she slid her arm around the boy's shoulders and tugged him into the seat next to her. "I'm glad they brought you here. I wasn't sure if that would happen and I couldn't figure out how I was going to get to you." That was a lie, but the last thing Ivy wanted was for Josh to assume she'd wiped her hands of him. "Who brought you here?"

Josh pointed at the tall man standing at the edge of the worried crew. "He did. He made me ride with him even though I didn't know if it was the right thing to do."

Glenn Earnshaw, one of Max's longtime friends and a great worker, seemed to sense Ivy and Josh were talking about him because he turned in their direction.

"Hey, Glenn." Ivy did her best to hold it together, barely managing to refrain from bursting into tears. "Thanks for bringing Josh here."

"I didn't have a choice." Glenn was calm, collected. "We shut down the lumberyard. We have to wait for OSHA to come by for an inspection. We can't do anything anyway until we're cleared."

"What's OSHA?" Josh asked.

"Occupational Safety and Health Administration," Ivy explained. "They have to make sure nobody was negligent at the lumberyard."

"Max is always stringent about safety guidelines," Glenn offered. "I'm sure it was some random accident that couldn't be avoided."

"I'm sure it was, too." Ivy was thoughtful as she ran her fingers through Josh's soft hair. "I still don't think I understand what happened, though. Did anyone see it?"

Glenn shrugged, noncommittal. "I don't know what we saw. We were outside and Max was showing Josh how some of the equipment worked. He obviously couldn't get close for safety purposes, but we managed to get him to a good vantage point.

"Max demonstrated how some of the bigger equipment worked and then he was hanging with Josh a bit and explaining things to him because he had a lot of questions," he continued. "After that Max went to talk to a few of the guys by a load that was due to be shipped out later in the day. That's when it happened."

"And the logs somehow just came loose?" Ivy had trouble believing that. Max was a stickler for making sure things like that never happened. Accidents couldn't always be avoided, of course, but Ivy was convinced there had to be more to the story. "That doesn't seem possible."

"I don't know what to tell you." Glenn dragged a restless hand through his hair. "It was weird. We didn't have any warning. We always check stuff like that. I have no idea why the strap broke. It's never happened to us before."

"It's just ... so weird." Ivy realized she was fretting – and in a manner that was likely to upset Josh – so she forced a wan smile and focused on the boy. "You weren't close to the area when it happened, were you?"

"No." Josh shook his head. "I was close to the logs before, but I was over on the other side when it happened. I guess I was lucky I wasn't killed, huh?"

Ivy had no idea what to make of the boy's blasé attitude. He didn't appear upset in the least by the potential tragedy. "I think we're all lucky because that didn't happen."

"Yeah. I didn't want to be at the lumberyard anyway. I wanted Max to take me to the nursery, but he said he couldn't and that I was stuck with him for the day."

"Yes, well, Max is fun," Ivy argued. "You should always want to spend time with him."

"I would rather spend time with you."

"I ... ." Ivy floundered, unsure how to soothe the boy while keeping her own emotions in check. "You're safe," she said finally. "That's the most important thing."

"It is," Josh agreed, amiable. "Can we go to the nursery now? I want to work on the plants again. I liked that."

Incredulity crawled through Ivy's belly like an army of invading ants. "We can't leave," she said, shaking her head. "We have to see how Max is doing."

"Why?"

"Because he was hurt."

"But why do we have to stay?" Josh queried. "Can't the hospital just call and tell us if he dies? I don't see why we have to wait here."

Uneasiness sat like an anvil on Ivy's diminutive shoulders as she eyed Josh, an emotion she couldn't quite identify causing annoyance to flare. "No. We can't leave and wait for a call. Besides that, Max isn't going to die."

"You don't know that." Josh barely showed any emotion as he met Ivy's steely gaze. "My father said my mother wouldn't die ... but she did. My father said he wouldn't leave me after that ... but he did. You can't stop people from leaving you."

The leading edge of Ivy's anger dissipated when she realized, in Josh's world, people almost always died. He didn't know any different. That wasn't his fault. He didn't realize what he was saying. "Max isn't going to die." She had faith that was true. "I'm sorry for what happened to you, but this is an entirely different situation. Max is going to be okay."

"I hope you're right. I like him."

"I know I'm right." Ivy was firm. "Now, you're going to have to sit here and wait with us. I'm sorry but ... we'll figure things out as soon as we get word on Max."

"That's fine." Josh tilted his head to the side as he smiled. "As long as we're together, I'm fine with anything."

JACK ARRIVED NOT LONG after Ivy gave Josh a coloring book – something he sneered at – and demanded he keep himself busy. The boy, however damaged, was starting to grate. She could understand why so many people referred to him as "needy." He clearly couldn't handle being on his own for an extended period of time.

"You made it." Ivy was relieved when she saw Jack, hopping to her feet and throwing her arms around his neck. "I wasn't sure if you would be able to get away."

"Nothing in this world could keep me from you in a situation like this." Jack calmly rubbed the back of Ivy's neck as he searched the waiting room. "Where are your parents?"

"Over there." Ivy pointed at the corner where Michael dragged Luna upon her arrival. She was so worked up that Michael was convinced she would cause a scene and he was trying to calm her down.

"Are you okay?" Jack kept his fingers busy. He could feel the knots of tension in Ivy's back and he was determined to give her what she needed even if she fought the effort.

"I'm fine. I'm not the one who was hurt."

Jack knew that wasn't true. "Have you heard any news?"

"Not yet."

"Well, I'm sure it will happen soon." Needing to offer love and support, Jack pulled Ivy into his arms and swayed back and forth as he studied the lobby. It was filled with people waiting to hear word about Max. Some of the people Jack didn't recognize. It was clear they were from the lumberyard. They were obviously as worked up as Ivy and the rest of the Morgan family. "It's going to be okay." He kissed Ivy's forehead before flicking his eyes to the sofa, surprise rushing through him when he caught sight of Josh. "Hey, buddy. What are you doing here?"

Josh was a kid caught in an untenable position. He merely shrugged when meeting Jack's gaze, his discomfort at the situation obvious. "Max took me to the lumberyard for the day. I was with him when it happened."

"He took you to the lumberyard?" Jack's eyebrows migrated north. That was news to him. "I didn't know he was doing that."

"He wanted to help." Ivy's voice cracked as she struggled to hold it together. "We thought it was a good idea. We had no idea this would happen."

"Oh, it's not your fault." Jack thought his heart might break at her expression. "Don't blame yourself. It's okay."

Ivy clung to him as the tears overflowed. She fought to keep from giving in to her fear for so long that she thought she'd won the war. It was obvious by the sobs wracking her body, though, that wasn't true. "I need him to be okay."

"He's going to be okay." Jack kissed her brow and cheek as he tightened his grip on her. "You'll see. His head is too hard to crack."

"You've got that right," Brian said, appearing at his partner's side and giving Ivy a sympathetic smile. "Max will be okay. I've known him for a very long time. He's not going to fall victim to something as simple as sliding logs."

"I hope so." Ivy pressed her head to Jack's chest. "We were together this morning. We spent hours having a morel-hunting competition. I won and he was furious. I promised to make his favorite mushroom gravy to ease the sting of the loss."

"You guys are so weird." Jack barked out a laugh. "I never knew morels were such a big deal until I moved up here. I don't get it."

"Morels are a way of life up here," Brian explained. "As far as Michiganders in this part of the state are concerned, there are only two types of people. There are morel lovers and people who should be booted from the state."

Jack scowled. "Nice. How come I only think you're saying that because I don't happen to like morels?"

"Because you're not that bright." Brian winked to let his partner know he was kidding. "As for the morels, now that I've heard that story I know Max will be fine. There's no way he'll allow Ivy to be the ultimate winner. That's not how he's built."

"That's true." Ivy was weary so she simply let Jack hold her while standing in the middle of the lobby, not caring in the least who was watching them. "We have to get Josh back to the home. I have no idea how long we're going to be here with Max, but we can't keep him here for this."

Josh immediately balked even though Ivy thought she uttered the words in a low enough voice that he wouldn't hear. "I want to stay here with you."

"You can't," Ivy protested. "I might be here all night."

"Then I want to stay all night."

"That's not possible, buddy," Jack said, hoping he sounded pragmatic rather than annoyed. He honestly wasn't sure which emotion was fueling him. "We can't keep you. We'll get in trouble. You have to go back to the home."

"I'll take him," Brian volunteered, taking Jack and Ivy by surprise.

"You don't have to do that," Ivy argued. "We're the ones who collected him from the home. It's our responsibility to take him back."

"I want to take him." Brian's tone was firm, making Ivy realize he wasn't going to back down. "It will be good for Josh and me to spend some time together. I have a few more questions about what happened that day in the woods and we can get them out of the way this afternoon."

Josh looked less than thrilled at the prospect. "Do I have to?" He turned a pleading set of eyes to Ivy. "Can't I just stay here with you?"

"I wish you could," Ivy replied. "It's not healthy for you to be here, though. I wasn't joking when I said that we might be here all night. I can't leave Max."

"But ... why?" Josh wrinkled his nose. "What good will it do for you to stay here? You can't help him."

"No, but I can be here for him."

"That doesn't help." Josh's belligerence was on full display. "Trust me. I was with my mother, but she died anyway. The same will probably happen to Max."

The words were like a kick in the gut to Ivy. "You don't mean that."

"I do." Josh was solemn. "I've seen it happen."

Jack recognized when a conversation was about to go off the rails and he was determined to keep that from happening. "We're all very sorry about what happened to you. Max's situation is different, though. I happen to think it's a good idea for Brian to take you back to the home."

"We'll be in touch," Brian promised, resting his hand on Josh's shoulder and giving the boy a pointed look. "We'll tell you when Max is doing better."

Josh looked as if he wanted to argue further, but a quick glance at all the stern faces surrounding him was proof that was a bad idea. "Fine." He heaved out a long-suffering sigh. "Let's go back to the home. I can't wait to go back to the worst place in the world."

Brian refused to let Josh bait him. "There are worse places. Trust me. Now ... come on. This isn't a healthy place for you to be."

"I've spent a lot of time in hospitals."

"That's why it's time to get you out of here." Brian refused to back down. "Let's go, kid. I'll buy you some ice cream on the way out of town."

Josh brightened considerably. "Can I have whatever I want?"

"Yup."

"Then let's get out of here."

Fourteen

Dr. Martin Nesbitt headed straight for Ivy and Jack when he hit the lobby. Michael and Luna scrambled in that direction, causing him to raise an eyebrow when everyone crowded around him.

"How is he?" Jack asked, keeping his arms tight around Ivy in case the news wasn't good. "He's going to be okay, isn't he?"

"He should be fine," Nesbitt replied, smiling in a reassuring manner. "He has a concussion and needs to be monitored for at least twenty-four hours, but he's regained consciousness and other than a few bumps and bruises, he's pretty much his normal self."

Ivy exhaled heavily. Even though she was trying to put a brave face on her fear, part of her was terrified that Max would never recover. "He's really okay?"

"He's hitting on the nurses."

Despite the serious nature of the situation, Ivy couldn't stop herself from giggling. "That sounds just like him. I'm sure he'll milk this for weeks."

"I'm sure he will, too," Luna agreed, pressing her hand to the spot above her heart. "He can milk it for as long as he wants as far as I'm concerned. I'm just glad he's going to be okay."

"He should be fine," Nesbitt reiterated. "I am keeping him here overnight for observation. He's not happy about that, but I figured you would handle making him fall into line, Luna."

"Oh, I'll definitely handle that. I'm staying with him, too. He may be an adult, but he's still my baby."

Michael smiled indulgently at his wife. "We'll both stay with him."

"I can make that happen," Nesbitt said agreeably. "If you're around he'll have no choice but to behave himself."

"What about after tonight?" Ivy asked, her mind already working. "Should he be at home alone? He can stay with us if he needs to be watched."

"He should be fine," Nesbitt countered. "I doubt very much he's going to want to stay with you. When I was asking him questions to make sure he hadn't forgotten anything, you were one of the first people I brought up. Do you know what he said?"

"I'm sure it had something to do with me being the best sister in the world," Ivy answered without hesitation, causing everyone to chuckle.

"Close." Nesbitt grinned at her. "I asked who Ivy Morgan was. He said she was his baby sister and she thought she was the queen of the world because she found more morels than him this morning. He also said she gets a goofy smile on her face whenever her handsy fiancé is around and he can barely watch without throwing up. I doubt very much he's going to want to stay with you given that."

"Ha, ha." Ivy rolled her eyes, although she was so happy with Max's prognosis that she couldn't put a lot of effort behind it. "Can I see him?"

"I don't see why not." Nesbitt gave her shoulder a squeeze. "Your parents are spending the night with him but keep your visit to a minimum. I want him to sleep as much as possible over the next twelve hours. Max should be back to his usual annoying self after that, though. You only need to take it easy on him for a little bit."

"She'll take it easy on him for at least a week," Luna warned, giving her daughter a pointed look. "She's going to let Max run her ragged if he needs it."

"Yes, mother, I'm aware of how your mind works when one of us is sick," Ivy supplied. "You don't have to worry. I'm going to spoil Max just as much as you."

"Good." Luna beamed. "You should go in and see him now. After that, I want his room to be a quiet place for him to rest and relax."

"Perhaps you should have him do some meditation," Ivy suggested, internally grinning at the thought. Max hated being quiet and their mother's idea of spiritual meditation was akin to torture for him. "I think that would really benefit him and his head injury."

Luna's smile was so wide it threatened to swallow her entire face. "That's a great idea."

"I'm glad you approve."

JACK WENT WITH IVY to visit Max, mostly because he wanted to be there in case Ivy started crying thanks to an emotional breakdown that he was convinced was going to happen regardless but also because he wanted to ask him a few questions. The minute he laid eyes on the older Morgan sibling, though, Jack knew he wouldn't press him too hard on the accident.

"You look awful," Ivy announced, striding to her brother's bedside.

"Thanks, Ivy," Max said dryly, his face ridiculously pale against the shock of dark hair feathered out against the pillow. "That's exactly what I want to hear."

"She didn't mean that," Jack said hurriedly. "She's been worried about you."

"Oh, I meant it." Ivy sat in the chair closest to the bed. "You look like an accountant spending time on the beach for the first time in a decade you're so white."

"That's ... heartening." Max smiled as he rested his hand on top of hers. "I'm sorry if I worried you."

"It goes along with the job of being a little sister. You worry about me, too."

"All of the time," Max confirmed. "Like, for example, when you were here almost a year ago after you were shot. That was no fun. This is no fun either, but I swear I'm going to be okay."

"I wasn't shot shot," Ivy countered. "I was only shot a little."

"That's not how I remember it."

"Me either," Jack muttered, his cheeks flushing with shame at the memory. Ivy was shot on what was essentially their second date and instead of standing with her while she recovered he ran like a coward. He still wasn't over it, although Ivy didn't appear to be holding a grudge. "Let's not talk about that," Jack insisted.

"Let's not," Max agreed. "It makes me want to punch you and I don't think I'm up to doing that today."

"Today?" Ivy made an exaggerated face. "You're going to be under Mom's special care for at least a week. You'd better brace yourself for that."

"She'll let it go once I return to work."

"I don't know how soon that's going to be," Ivy hedged. "Glenn said OSHA is going to have to clear things before you can start up again. I'm guessing that's going to be a few days."

"I'll get on them tomorrow." Max didn't look overly worried, but Ivy could sense the nerves coursing through him. "It will be fine."

"Do you know what happened?" Jack asked, moving to stand next to Ivy's chair. "My understanding is that a strap holding together some logs broke free and that's how you were injured. I would think that's not a normal occurrence."

"No, definitely not normal," Max agreed. "I'm not sure what happened. I test those straps every week. Anything that looks like it's going to give gets tossed. The good news is, it wasn't the really big logs we get for log cabin builds. It was a smaller pile."

"I don't know that I feel better about that," Ivy noted. "You still could've been killed."

"I wasn't, though. I'm too handsome to die." Max winked for good measure. "I'm going to be fine. I was more worried about Josh. The doctor didn't know what happened to him. Please tell me he wasn't too traumatized."

"I think the problem is that Josh is traumatized by previous stuff," Jack answered. "He seems ... weird ... sometimes. I think he's screwed up in the head when it comes to normal human reactions."

"Can you blame him?" Max challenged. "He's lost his mother and father."

"And an infant sister who died of SIDS," Jack added. "He lost the sister first and she simply slipped away in her sleep. Since there's no acceptable explanation for why something like that happens, I'm guessing Josh has been struggling with questions ever since."

"From what you told me, I'm guessing his mother and father were struggling to find answers themselves and let him fall by the wayside as they shut down a bit," Ivy added. "I don't blame them. They were going through a lot and it was understandable how distracted they were. However, I don't think they did Josh any favors."

"How was he with you at the lumberyard today?" Jack asked his future brother-in-law, genuinely curious. "Did he give you any grief? He wasn't thrilled when Brian announced he was taking him back to the home. I thought he was going to melt down and start screaming at one point, but he managed to hold it together."

"He wasn't bad," Max supplied. "He wasn't exactly happy and ready to do cartwheels – he kept asking about Ivy and why she wasn't spending time with him – but he wasn't a monster or anything. I will say he has a curious mind. When I distracted him with equipment and the wood-bundling process certain orders go through, well, he was fascinated."

That didn't surprise Ivy in the least. "He was the same way at the nursery. Plus, the day we took him back to the cottage, he told us his father liked to show him how things on car engines work. I'm betting Abraham realized he had a scientific mind and tried to keep it engaged."

"Yes, well, I think Abraham was probably looking for anything he could find to keep Josh distracted," Jack countered. "I talked to Abraham's mistress today and she told me Josh walked in on her and his father – not naked but clearly in the midst of a heavy conversation – and he didn't take things well. He totally freaked."

Ivy was horrified. "Abraham took his girlfriend to his house knowing Josh could stumble across her at any time?"

"No, Melanie was in the hospital and Abraham called his mistress to end things and Josh walked in on it," Jack clarified. "I don't have time to tell the whole story – Dr. Nesbitt warned us we couldn't stay in here too long – but the mistress says that Abraham was trying to make things right for his family."

"Still, that couldn't have gone over well with Josh," Max pointed out. "His mother was dying and his father was spending all his time with another woman. It's no wonder the kid is so needy. He's used to people abandoning him ... or just plain neglecting him."

"He's definitely needy," Ivy agreed, rolling her neck. "His emotions are blunted, too. I think you were right about what you said yesterday, Jack. I think he's hiding something."

"I kind of want to make you speak into my phone and record you saying that," Jack said, his eyes twinkling. "The part about me being right, I mean."

Ivy made a disgusted face. "I admit when I'm wrong."

Jack and Max barked out twin guffaws.

"I do," Ivy persisted. "I'm not often wrong but, when I am, I admit it."

"Sure, honey." Jack snagged her hand and kissed the palm. "As for me being right, though, the more time I spend with Josh, the more I think I'm right, too. He's definitely hiding something."

"What is he hiding?" Max asked. "Do you think he knows who killed his father?"

"I do." Jack bobbed his head. "I think he knows and he's frightened. I also think that the mistress might know a little more than she's letting on. She admitted to being obsessed with Abraham and angry about him spending more time with his sick wife than her. I can't help but wonder if she might have a part in all this, although what that part might be is beyond me."

"How will you track it down?" Ivy asked.

"I don't know." Jack squeezed her hand. "For right now, I'm going to take you out to dinner and then go to bed early. I need a good night's sleep. I'm hopeful the answer will come to me in a dream."

Ivy's lips curved. She knew exactly what he was referring to. "Maybe it will."

"Ugh." Max slapped a hand over his eyes. "I don't want to see this. Dying would've been better than seeing this."

"Don't ever say anything like that again," Ivy warned, extending a finger. "I don't like it."

"Fine." Max snagged her finger and smirked. "I won't ever say anything like that again. I expect chocolate cake, morel soup, and cherry pie to make me feel better, though. That's the trade-off."

Ivy stared at him for a long beat. "Sold."

Max's grin widened. "I'm going to like you doting on me. I can already tell."

"Don't get used to it. In a week I'll forget that you almost died."

"Then it's going to be one heck of a week."

JACK MET IVY IN the woods by tacit agreement that night. Technically it was the dreamscape they shared, but he allowed her to build the world since she knew it best. It was a way for him to go over the scene again, this time allowing her to figure things out at his side.

"Is this how you remember it being?" Ivy asked. She wore simple cargo pants and a T-shirt in the dream, an outfit she wore often in the waking world, but Jack couldn't help being disappointed.

"I thought you were going to dress in something a little more ... fun," he complained, eliciting an eye roll from his fiancée.

"We're in the woods," Ivy pointed out. "I can't be naked in the woods. We'll stop by the beach on our way back and I'll get naked there."

"Good idea." Jack shot her an enthusiastic thumbs-up before scanning the clearing. Abraham Masters' body was back where they found it, although he opted not to spend too much time looking at the grisly wounds. It bothered him that Ivy had such strong mental recall and could see something so bloody with a clear head. "This is how I remember it. You didn't need to bring the body back, though."

"Oh." Ivy briefly closed her eyes, and when she opened them again, Abraham was gone. "Better?"

"Much better." Jack moved to where the body rested seconds before and turned to face her. "So, if Abraham was here and looking in your direction, you should be roughly standing where the assailant shot from."

"Okay." Ivy glanced behind her. "He must have come from those trees." She inclined her chin to the spot over her shoulder. "Otherwise they would've seen him coming from a long distance away. The trees aren't thick through here."

"Maybe." Jack wasn't convinced that was true. "Picture what was happening, though. Abraham and Josh were talking while walking. They weren't paying attention to their surroundings. I mean ... why would they? It shouldn't have been a dangerous outing. There was nothing out here to make Abraham fearful."

"So, what do you think happened?" Ivy asked. She found Jack's mind a wonder sometimes, especially when he was picking apart a crime scene.

"I think that Abraham recognized someone was approaching." Jack rubbed his chin as he swiveled to look in every direction. "I think he saw someone coming and probably even recognized him.

"Josh said his ears weren't working, which signifies to me that he was in shock before the shooting even happened," he continued. "I think Abraham was arguing with whoever approached and he yelled for Josh to run. The kid did what his father asked and probably heard a gunshot when he wasn't far off."

"But why lie about what he saw?" Ivy asked the obvious question. "Josh described a rifle."

"His father had a rifle," Jack reminded her. "What if Abraham had his gun pointed at the other man but never got a shot off? The man then shot Abraham, killed him, and collected Abraham's gun."

"Why do that when he could've claimed self-defense?"

"My guess is that whoever it was has ties to Ellen Woodbridge," Jack replied. "I'm thinking it was either a new boyfriend or a brother. She somehow convinced him to confront Abraham. It's hard to sell self-defense if you have a history with the man you killed."

"I can see that." Ivy pursed her lips. "How do you explain the difference in scenarios, though? I mean ... Josh described something totally different."

"Well, I've been thinking about that." Jack was somber. "Josh could've lied to protect himself. He was probably terrified. Once reality set in, he knew he couldn't take it back without looking bad. The kid has been through a lot and this is just the latest in a string of tragedies that have upended his life."

"So how should we approach it?"

"First thing tomorrow, I'm going to request a trauma therapist head to the children's home to meet with Josh," Jack replied without hesitation. "We need to get inside that kid's psyche. I think he knows who shot his father. We need to get him to admit he lied from the start."

"Is that the only way? What if he feels so much guilt he never owns up to it?"

"Then we start looking for the gun," Jack answered. "Abraham registered it. If someone tries to sell it – which would be the smart thing to do because being found with it would almost certainly signify guilt – we should be able to track down who sold it."

"That seems like a lot of work," Ivy hedged. "Can you get your hands on all those gun records?"

"I can try. Not all guns have to be registered. I'm more hopeful that whoever took it panicked and dropped it off at a pawnshop to get rid of it. He might not have been thinking at the time and that could be his downfall."

"That sounds like a plan." Ivy gave the clearing another look before extending her hand to Jack. "I never thought I would say this, but I'm tired of the woods. Let's go someplace tropical and put thoughts of this case behind us for a little bit."

Jack's eyebrow quirked. "Just focus on each other for a few hours?"

"That's the plan."

Jack took her hand and nodded. "That's the best offer I've had all day."

"You and me both."

Fifteen

"**H**ey."

Jack greeted Ivy's sleepy eyes with a smile as she slowly opened them the following morning.

"Hey." Ivy instinctively lifted a finger and rubbed it down his cheek. "You look like you got some sun."

Jack snorted. They spent hours frolicking on the beach in the dreamscape. She was obviously trying to be funny. "Yes. Since we were naked, though, I have no tan lines."

Ivy stared at him for a long beat. A slow starter, it often took her longer to register things when she first woke up. "You honestly look like you got some sun."

Jack scratched his cheek as he regarded her. Now that she mentioned it, she looked bronzer than normal herself. "Huh. You looked pretty healthy and robust, too."

Ivy narrowed her eyes. "What is that supposed to mean?"

"That you're pretty as a picture ... and you've got a bit of color to your cheeks," Jack replied without hesitation. He grabbed the covers and drew them back so he could look over Ivy's body. "Your legs look a bit darker, too."

Ivy glanced down and frowned. He wasn't wrong. She was a stickler about sunscreen. Often, by the end of summer, she had a decent amount of color, but she never sought it out. Since the only place she'd gone where she was exposed to the sun without sunscreen was the dreamscape, she was genuinely baffled. "What do you make of that?"

"I don't know." Jack flicked his eyes to his chest and ran his hands over the slight pink color – not enough sunburn to be painful, thankfully – he found there. "I'm tan, too."

"You went shirtless in the dream," Ivy pointed out, her fingertips landing on the top of Jack's scar. It was located close to his heart – in the spot where his former partner shot him – and he only went shirtless when it was just the two of them or they were in the dreamscape. He didn't want people asking about what happened to him. As a private person, explaining it was simply too much effort.

"I was." Jack rested his hand on top of hers and squeezed her fingers. "Maybe we're just imagining this."

"Maybe," Ivy said, although she wasn't convinced.

"Maybe it's psychosomatic," Jack suggested. "I mean ... we felt as if we were out in the sun and having a great day, so we convinced ourselves that was true and ended up with tans."

Ivy cocked a mocking eyebrow. "I'm not a doctor, but I don't think it works that way."

"Then you explain it," Jack prodded. "I know for a fact we didn't leave this bed last night. The only sun we saw was in our heads."

"I know." Ivy pulled herself to a sitting position and ran her fingers through her hair. "I don't know what to make of it. Yelling at me isn't going to help me come up with answers."

"That wasn't yelling." Jack made a face as he shifted to sit next to Ivy, resting his head against hers as he ran his hand over her back. "I didn't mean to upset you. I was just ... surprised."

"You and me both," Ivy said. "I don't know how to explain it. We've been to that beach in our dreams numerous times and this has never happened before."

"Maybe you're getting stronger."

Ivy swallowed hard. "You think I did this?"

Jack kissed her temple before answering. "I think, whether you like to admit it or not, you're capable of doing some fantastical things."

"This is different from the other stuff, though," Ivy argued. "Sharing dreams is weird, but it's not like this. This is ... freaky." She stared at her hands. "What's happening to me?"

"Oh, honey, I don't know." Jack's heart rolled at her worried expression. "This is not the end of the world. We'll just make a point to put on sunscreen next time in the dream. Since it's not real we can simply conjure it and it should work."

"We shouldn't have to do that. It's a dream, for crying out loud. The whole point is to be naked on a beach without a care in the world."

"Well, apparently now we have to care about sunscreen. It's not a big deal."

"It feels like a big deal."

"I know." Jack was uncertain how to soothe her. "It doesn't change anything, though. I love you because you're you. That's never going to change."

"You're not afraid?"

"Of you? Absolutely not. Am I afraid of other things? Yeah. That's human nature."

"What are you most afraid of?" Ivy was terrified to hear the answer, but she had to ask the question.

"Losing you," Jack replied without hesitation, causing her to jerk her head up in surprise. "I can survive a lot." He tapped the scar on his chest as proof. "I can't survive losing you, though. I'm most afraid that you'll find trouble and I won't get to you in time. That's what fuels my nightmares."

His honest answer threw Ivy for a loop. "I'm afraid to lose you, too."

"I think your fear stems from the fact that you think I'm going to run away if you keep manifesting odd abilities," Jack noted. "I need you to know, no matter what, that's not true. You can't shake me, honey. It's you and me together. Forever. No matter what."

Ivy mustered a genuine smile. "I actually knew that. Thanks for saying it, though. I kind of needed to hear it."

"I know." Jack pressed a soft kiss to her mouth. "I will say it again and again as long as you need to hear it."

"Once is good for today." Ivy grabbed both sides of his face and smacked a noisy kiss against his lips. "I'll always love you no matter what, too."

Jack grinned. "That's good to know."

"Yeah." They stared into each other's eyes for a long beat. Then the reality of the day set in. "I need to go to the lumberyard."

The conversational shift caught Jack off guard. "Why?"

"Because I want to look around and make sure there's no other accident waiting to happen," Ivy answered honestly. "Max will be back at the lumberyard tomorrow – no matter how my mother and father try to fight him – so I want to make sure everything there is okay. Er, if not okay at least not ready to fall apart. That business is his life and he loves it. I want to make sure something bigger isn't wrong."

"Like what?"

Ivy held her hands palms out and shrugged. "I don't know. I can't help thinking the timing was a bit convenient."

Jack stilled, legitimately surprised. "What do you mean?"

"I mean that I'm suspicious." Ivy saw no reason to lie. If Jack could put up with the fact that she gave them both a tan in their dreams, he wouldn't gripe about her admitting to what was really bothering her this morning. "I think that someone tried to hurt Max."

"Purposely hurt him?" Jack rubbed the back of his head as he regarded her. "Can you explain why you think that? I'm not saying I disagree," he added hurriedly. "I would simply like to understand how you came to that determination."

Ivy wasn't offended by the question. "Whatever you think about Max, he's not the lazy sort. He always follows safety protocol and doesn't put his men in danger. I've seen him test those straps. There's no way he used one that gave for no good reason."

"Okay." Jack ran his thumb over her cheek. She was so earnest it was likely to hurt his heart if he didn't agree with her. "Do you think one of his men went after him?"

Ivy vehemently shook her head. "I think it was someone else."

"Who?"

"Maybe it's the person who killed Abraham Masters."

Jack was officially flabbergasted. "I don't understand."

"You said that Josh knew who shot his father and didn't say something because he was afraid," Ivy pointed out. "Yesterday, at the hospital, I got a whiff of something when I touched Josh's arm. I didn't think anything of it at first. He was terrified, and I could feel it. I was too worried about Max to focus on it."

"Now that you know Max is going to make a full recovery, however, you've given it some thought," Jack prodded.

"Exactly." Ivy bobbed her head. "I think Josh saw something and he doesn't want to say what it is."

"What do you think he saw?"

"I don't know."

"Theorize."

"Okay." Ivy licked her lips as she gathered her thoughts. "What if someone has been following Josh this whole time to make sure he doesn't say anything? What if that someone watched Max and Josh yesterday and worried Josh might open up to my brother so he or she decided to send a message?"

"Well, it's an interesting thought." Jack rubbed his chin. "Do you think someone could pull that off without anyone noticing, though?"

"I talked to Glenn before you arrived. Everyone was watching Max demonstrate how to use the equipment. Everyone was focused in that direction. Someone could've easily snuck up and messed with the strap."

"Josh did say he was standing close to those logs earlier in the afternoon," Jack mused. "I guess it's not out of the realm of possibility. How are you going to handle this, though? Are you just going to wander around the lumberyard and touch things?"

"That's exactly what I'm going to do."

Jack wasn't happy with the admission. "I have some things to do this morning. I need to visit the state pathologist and see if we can go over Melanie Masters' records. I have some other calls to make. Do you think you can put off this trip until tomorrow?"

"No."

"Ivy ... ."

Ivy held up her hand to still him. "I need to check things out. I have to see for myself. No one is going to be over there. It's not as if whoever did this – and technically we don't know that anyone really did this – is going to be at the lumberyard. It would be a waste of time for someone to hang out there. It's obvious that Josh isn't going to be visiting the lumberyard today."

"That's true," Jack muttered, not entirely placated. "I don't like the idea of you going over there alone, though."

"I'm going to be there for ten minutes," Ivy pointed out. "I'll be fine. Trust me. If I can give myself a tan in my dreams, I can keep myself safe at the lumberyard no one knows I'm going to visit."

Jack ran his hand over her hair to smooth it. "I'm still not happy with your plan."

"I'll text you when I land and when I leave."

"Better, but I would prefer you wait for me."

"I can't do that." Ivy was firm. "I'm going to have Dad pick up Josh and bring him to the nursery, which means I need to get my visit to the lumberyard over early so I can focus on Josh."

"And why are you going to bring Josh to the nursery again?" Jack queried, his irritation coming out to play. "I thought you agreed that spending a lot of time with him was a bad idea."

"I do agree that him getting attached to me is a bad idea," Ivy countered. "At this point, I think spending time with him will help. I'm the only one who can get the truth out of him."

Despite himself, Jack was intrigued. "And what do you think the truth is?"

"I think that you're right about him knowing who killed his father," Ivy answered. "I think he knows and he's absolutely terrified to tell us. He trusts me, though, so he's far more likely to confide in me. The second he does, we can go after this person – whoever it is – and get Josh placed in a permanent home."

"Will you still visit him after that?" Jack was honestly curious. "I mean ... will you stick with him even after he admits he lied?"

"Yes." Ivy bobbed her head. "We both know he lied because he was afraid. He's basically lost everyone who ever meant anything to him. The only thing he has left to hold on to is his own life. I don't blame him for being terrified enough to spin a tall tale."

"I don't either," Jack admitted. "Basically I'm working on the assumption that this all dates back to Abraham's affair with Ellen. I mean ... she said the right things. She said that she was over him and realized, at least in hindsight, that she was acting like a dolt.

"There was something about the way she said it that bothered me," he continued. "It was as if she wanted to appear sincere, proactive with her guilt even, but couldn't quite pull it off."

"So ... you think she has something to do with this?" Ivy pressed.

"I think she at least knows more than she's letting on," Jack replied. "There was something off about her demeanor that I couldn't quite identify. I don't know what her deal was, but I'm convinced she didn't tell us all that she knows."

"She could've convinced someone to go after Abraham," Ivy pointed out. "I mean ... think about it. She probably thought he would turn to her once Melanie died, start their affair all over again. When that didn't happen, it could've legitimately turned her bitter."

"And I'm guessing that's exactly what happened," Jack said. "We know that Josh saw Ellen at least once. He walked into his home and saw his father with his mistress. The way Ellen made it sound, nothing was going on. What if that wasn't true?"

Ivy leaned forward, intrigued. "What do you mean?"

"Well, this is also just a theory, but what if Abraham and Ellen were actually saying goodbye to one another in a different way?"

"You mean a naked goodbye?"

Jack nodded and smirked. "Exactly. What if Josh saw them, pitched a fit, and Abraham cut Ellen loose because his son was so upset, not because he was trying to do right by his wife, like Ellen said."

"Huh." Ivy tapped her chin as she mulled the scenario. "That actually fits together."

"It does," Jack agreed. "The only thing that doesn't fit is the actual shooting. Ellen isn't very big. I don't see her being able to contain Abraham and Josh."

"If she's the guilty party, though, she would've had a gun."

"True," Jack agreed. "Why would Ellen want to kill Abraham? Wouldn't it make more sense for her to want to kill Josh? He was the one she most likely blamed for her relationship with Abraham falling apart."

"Good point." Ivy bopped her head, as if listening to music only she could hear. "Maybe she has a boyfriend who helped. A brother, perhaps."

"I've considered that, too, and I'm researching both today," Jack said. "That's another reason I can't go to the lumberyard with you."

Ivy's expression was rueful as she patted his arm. "Do you really think I can't visit the lumberyard without something happening to me?"

"I really think trouble seems to find you no matter how good you intend on being," Jack countered. "Sometimes I think you exert a musk that attracts killers and thieves."

"Too bad I couldn't reverse engineer that, huh?" Ivy's eyes sparkled. "I would be rich beyond our wildest dreams if I could come up with a perfume that kept bad people from good people."

"Oh, I think you hit on something there." Jack grinned as he wrapped his arms around her waist and wrestled her to the bed. "I think you should focus on that and not leave the house today. Make us rich, honey. Then neither of us will have to work and we can spend the rest of our lives in bed."

"Ha, ha." Ivy kissed his chin. "I have to go to the lumberyard. I also have to focus on Josh to see if I can get him to talk. He's our best hope of getting answers."

"I know." Jack was resigned. "I don't like worrying about you, though. It makes me edgy."

"I already said I would text to let you know when I arrive and leave. I promise I won't be there long."

"Text me a couple of times when you hit the nursery, too," Jack instructed. "That way I'll know you're safe."

Ivy snorted. "Dad is going to be at the nursery with me. Plus ... well ... all the customers. Who do you think is going to go after me there?"

"Probably no one," Jack conceded. "That doesn't mean I'm going to stop worrying about you. That's not how I roll."

"Oh, I know how you roll." Ivy poked his side. "You like to roll around with me in the sand."

"You've got that right." Jack kissed her again. "Just promise me you'll take care of yourself, always look over your back, and text a lot.

That won't stop me from worrying, but it will help ... at least a little bit."

"I promise to do all that." Ivy was sincere. "I also promise to come up with a few dirty texts to send your way."

Jack's eyes gleamed with interest. "There's a reason I'm so in love with you. The dirty texts play into it."

Ivy chuckled. "I love you, too. Outrageously."

"I don't suppose you have a few minutes to show me before you leave for the day, do you?" Jack glanced at the clock on the nightstand. "I think, if properly motivated, we can figure out a way to forget our problems for the next fifteen minutes."

"I love it when I'm properly motivated," Ivy enthused.

"Me, too." Jack smacked a kiss against her lips. "Let's see who can motivate who, huh?"

"That sounds like a plan to me."

Sixteen

Ivy was quick when she landed at the lumberyard, parking her car in Max's reserved spot and hurrying across the untidy landscape. It was obvious where the accident happened and she wasn't keen to spend a lot of time wondering what might've happened to Max if the accident went down a different way.

Since Ivy spent a lot of time with her brother at his place of business, she knew how to navigate the area with safety in mind. She gave the various piles of wood long looks before passing in front of them and didn't stop until she found the scattered logs in the middle of the aisle.

Right away, Ivy could tell where they were stored. They were obviously tied together for a specific purpose – probably to be shipped within the next twenty-four hours or so – and were meant to be largely ignored until they were transported off the lot.

Thankfully for all concerned – especially Max – the logs weren't overly large. Even though she didn't consider herself a master builder by any stretch of the imagination, Ivy recognized what the logs were going to be used for. They were completely straight and cut to the same length. That meant they were going to be roof pieces, most likely for a log cabin. There were a lot of expensive log cabins going up in the area, so it made sense.

Ivy was careful as she climbed over two logs, keeping her eyes peeled on the ground until she found what she was looking for. It was the tie from the end of the stack. It looked to be in one piece, perhaps dislodged when the other end opened and the stack rolled.

Even though Ivy wasn't convinced she could command full use of her magic when she wanted to do it, she focused on the tie now, closing her eyes and breathing in through her nose as she tried to relax her mind. She knew exactly what she was looking for. Unfortunately for her, the images she hoped to see didn't come through.

"Well, that bites," Ivy muttered under her breath as she shoved the tie in her pocket and scrambled over the logs. She kept her eyes on the ground, determined to find the second tie. She almost missed it, but a hint of color poking out from the far end of one of the logs caught her attention. The second Ivy scooped it up, a myriad of images flashed through her head, each darker than the previous.

At first, Ivy didn't understand what she was seeing. When things slipped into place, however, she was appropriately horrified.

"Oh, no." She had no idea how long she was trapped in the vision stream, but when she snapped out of it, she jumped to her feet. "Oh, no, no, no, no."

MICHAEL DIDN'T HAVE A PROBLEM picking up Josh when Ivy called to ask him for a favor. In truth, he felt for the boy. He couldn't imagine going through the terrible things plaguing Josh's life at such a young age.

The boy had lost a sister to SIDS, something that defied understanding. Then he watched his mother suffer and slip away. Then, only a year later, someone took his father in brutal fashion. A sympathetic man at heart, Michael couldn't understand why everything was piling on Josh, and seemingly in such a short time span. How much was one boy supposed to survive? Especially now that he was on his own.

"Thank you for picking me up." Josh was in polite mode as Michael navigated through downtown Shadow Lake. "Where is Ivy that she couldn't do it?"

"I'm actually not completely sure," Michael replied. "I know she's on her way out to the nursery, but she said she had somewhere to be before then."

"And where is that?"

"I don't know but ... oh, look." Michael pointed toward the medical center as they passed. "That's Ivy's car right there. She must be visiting Max. I had no idea she planned to do that today."

Josh craned his neck so he could stare at the hospital. "They're close, huh?"

"Who? Max and Ivy?" Michael smiled at mention of his children. "They are pretty close."

"Max is older?"

"He is."

"Did he like Ivy when you brought her home from the hospital?"

The question caught Michael off guard. "I think he did. He wasn't very old when it happened. He was two – more like two and a half, I guess – and he was fascinated with watching her."

"But he liked her?"

Michael nodded, something occurring to him. "I know you had a sister."

"You know about her?" Josh seemed surprised. "No one ever talked about her after she died. Not really. I knew my mother was sad, which I didn't get because it's not like she had Jenny all that long, but no one talked about her out in the open or anything."

Michael was surprised by Josh's matter-of-fact demeanor. "Well, my guess is that your parents were so upset about what happened to Jenny that they couldn't find the right words to express the emotions they were grappling with. How can you explain something that has no rhyme or reason?"

"She didn't do anything, though," Josh persisted. "She just sat in that crib and cried. She cried all the time. Mom said it was normal, but she just wouldn't shut up."

Michael was taken aback by Josh's tone. "That's what babies do.

They cry. Eventually they grow out of it, but that's the only way an infant can communicate."

"Did Max like it when Ivy cried?"

Michael had no idea why Josh was so fixated on Max. It seemed like an odd question to ask, although harmless, so he answered it all the same. "Max didn't like it when Ivy cried."

"Did he ask you to shut her up?"

"No. It was more that he kind of wrung his hands and got nervous when she cried. He was always afraid something was wrong with her. Even at two he was a good big brother and told us to go to her when she was upset. He always put her first."

"I didn't feel that way about Jenny." Josh's expression was a mix between a scowl and a sneer. "I just wanted her to be quiet. I told Mom that, but she said I was being ridiculous and to go outside if the noise bothered me that much. I never got to sleep through the entire night after they brought Jenny home. It was ... terrible."

"Well, I'm sure it was." Michael chose his words carefully. "Still, she would've grown out of that. Eventually you wouldn't even have remembered that she used to cry so often."

"Oh, I would've remembered."

Michael cleared his throat to dislodge some of the discomfort rolling through him. "Still, you must have missed her once she was gone."

"No. We didn't have her very long. It was just like going back to how things were supposed to be before they brought her home from the hospital."

Michael was utterly flabbergasted. "You can't mean that. She was your sister."

"I think it's probably different for people like Max and Ivy," Josh offered, taking on a pragmatic tone. "They were close in age. Max was too young to realize he had it better before Ivy was born. It was different for me."

"Yeah. I'm starting to see that."

Josh rested his hands on his knees and turned a bright, if somewhat vacant, smile in Michael's direction. "Can we get ice cream before heading out?"

"Sure," Michael replied, conflicted. "I think ice cream will do us both good."

MAX WAS SURPRISED TO FIND Ivy waiting for him when he exited his hospital room's private bathroom in street clothes.

"I thought Mom was coming," he said as he slid into his weathered hoodie. "Don't tell me she's already tired of serving as my nurse because I've come up with a whole list of things I want her to do before I'm going to be feeling well enough to take care of myself."

Ivy scowled, understanding exactly what her brother had planned for their long-suffering mother. "Ugh. You're going to make her clean your house and find someone to dress up like a naughty nurse for you, aren't you?"

Max was appalled. "I would never have Mom pick out a naughty nurse for me. I'm going to make Jack do that. He knows who would look good in the little uniform and I'm sure he would be open to holding auditions."

"Over my dead body."

Max smirked, genuinely amused. "That might be fun to watch. I honestly haven't ruled it out."

"Whatever."

"For now, I'm simply curious," Max said. "What are you doing here?"

"I stopped by the lumberyard," Ivy replied, digging in her pocket. "I was looking for these." She dropped the ties she found into his hand, watching as Max wrinkled his nose while studying them. "What do you see?"

"These are log ties."

"I know that."

"This one has been cut," Max noted, his cheeks flushing with color as he studied the item in question.

"Are you sure it was cut?" Ivy pressed. She already suspected that, but Max was an expert and she wanted him to verify it for her. "You're absolutely positive that it was cut and didn't somehow break from natural causes, right?"

"Do you see this?" Max pointed at the edge of the broken tie. "If it ripped, it would be jagged. This isn't jagged."

"No, it's not." Ivy dragged a hand through her hair as she began to pace in front of the bed.

"What are you thinking?" Max asked, concern for his sister outweighing his fury over the sabotaged tie. "You know something, don't you?"

"I don't know anything," Ivy countered. "I suspect something, though."

"That's the same thing."

"Not really."

Ivy made a "well, duh" expression as she rolled her eyes. "I don't know anything," she reiterated. "However, I saw something when I touched the tie. It was fast ... basically a flash ... but I saw something."

"Is this that magical witchy thing you've been doing where you see things that no one else can see?" Max asked.

"Kind of. If you're going to give me grief about it, save it. I already know you think I'm nuts."

"I don't think you're nuts," Max countered. "I don't think you're even remotely nuts."

"So ... what do you think?"

"I think you're special and that you can do things," Max replied without hesitation. "I don't know why you can do these things and I can't – it would be totally awesome if I had magic and we both know it – but I have faith you're powerful. Just tell me what you saw."

Ivy heaved out a sigh as she collected herself. "I went in thinking that I was going to see a stranger cutting the tie. That somehow, when you were distracted by the machinery, someone snuck close enough to cut the tie in an effort to either hurt Josh or send him a warning."

"Jack's still convinced he's lying about what happened in the woods, isn't he?"

Ivy nodded. "He *is* lying about what happened in the woods." She was sure of that now. "I thought I would see someone else cutting the tie at the lumberyard, Max, but I didn't. Josh is the one who did it."

Max wasn't sure what he was expecting his sister to say, but that wasn't it. "You can't be serious."

"I am, and I'm starting to think he was the one who shot his father."

"No way." Max thought back to the kid who came running through the woods. "I can't believe that."

"I think I have a way to check," Ivy persisted, grabbing Max's hand and giving it a squeeze. "I need you to come with me to be sure, though."

"Absolutely." Max didn't hesitate, instead pulling on his shoes. "I want to know the truth as much as you. It could be important when it comes to my meeting with OSHA."

"Then let's go. Dad is taking Josh to the nursery. I want to check my hunch before confronting him."

"That sounds like a plan to me."

THE STATE PATHOLOGIST was an older woman – she had to be pushing sixty and looked tired – but she offered Jack a bright smile when he sat across from her desk. He'd gone out of his way to drive to the Grayling post so he could talk to the woman directly. After all, she was the one who made the final ruling on Melanie Masters' death.

"Thank you for taking time to see me," Jack started. "I know this is probably not how you wanted to spend your day – going over an old case and bringing up closed files – but I really appreciate you taking the time."

Addison Strawser waved off Jack's concern and merely smiled. "That's my job, son. Besides, I was expecting someone to ask further questions about this one eventually. I figured it was only a matter of time."

Jack inched forward on his chair. "What do you mean by that? You didn't seem surprised when I called this morning and asked to go over your findings a second time. I found that ... curious."

"That's because I wasn't surprised," Strawser explained. "I always knew my decision on this case would come back to haunt me."

"And, if I'm understanding things correctly, your decision was that Melanie Masters wasn't poisoned, correct?"

"Actually, I found inconclusive results on that front," Strawser replied. "I couldn't find anything that pointed toward a specific toxin. Melanie Masters was very clearly sick, and something was eating away at her from the inside. The doctors couldn't find what that something was, though. When it came time for an autopsy and tests, I couldn't find the reason either."

Jack was flustered. "But you have suspicions, don't you?"

Strawser heaved out a sigh. "I do. I think she was poisoned. Although, I have no idea what poisoned her. In truth, I was leaning toward a particular toxin, rather than a poison, but backed off at the last minute because it was a theory rather than fact."

"Well, I'm willing to listen to your theory," Jack said. "Abraham Masters was killed in Shadow Lake a few days ago and it's looking more and more likely that his death is somehow tied to that of his wife. I need to know what you suspected if I hope to untangle all of this."

"Okay, but just remember, it's nothing I can testify to in court," Strawser warned. "I believe that Melanie Masters was poisoned with false morels."

Jack blinked several times in rapid succession. "You mean ... mushrooms?"

"Yes. Do you know what morels are?"

Jack barked out a hollow laugh. "I do. My fiancée is obsessed with the things. I don't happen to be a fan, but she loves them."

"Yes, well, real morels are delicious and even healthy. False morels are another story."

"I guess I don't understand." Jack shifted in his chair. "How can you tell the difference?"

"True morel hunters know. They know to avoid them, at least. Let me guess, did your fiancée search through your bag before cooking up anything you collected?"

"How did you know she made me go mushroom hunting with her?"

"Morel hunting is a sport to people up here," Strawser replied. "It's basically an Olympic sport. Other people don't get it but those interested in medaling understand exactly what they're doing."

"Well, okay. Now that you mention it, Ivy did search through the morels I found. It wasn't a lot anyway. She's much better at spotting them than I am. She threw a couple away."

"I'm going to guess those were false morels," Strawser said. "The thing is, false morels look a lot like real morels but are easy to separate if you pay attention."

"And false morels are poisonous?"

"Oh, yes." Strawser bobbed her head. "The toxins from false morels can stay in your system for a long time. The mushrooms themselves are tasty and go down smooth – at least if you like regular morels, which it sounds like you don't – but they can kill you."

"Do you think Melanie Masters was fed false morels over an extended period of time?"

"I think Melanie Masters was likely fed small doses of false morels to keep her sick," Strawser corrected. "I don't have proof of that, though. There was nothing in her autopsy report to prove that beyond a shadow of a doubt."

"Abraham Masters was a morel enthusiast," Jack noted, his mind busy as he mulled a myriad of possibilities. "He was out in the woods hunting for them when he was shot. I'm assuming he was your prime suspect when you came up with the false morel theory."

"More often than not it's always the spouse who is considered to be the primary suspect," Strawser supplied. "Like I said, I don't have proof that he did anything in this particular case."

"Yeah, but you strongly suspect." Things were starting to come together for Jack and he didn't like the way the puzzle looked now that pieces were snapping into place. "I wonder if Josh Masters knew what his father did to his mother."

"I don't know how he would figure something like that out," Strawser countered. "My understanding is that he's a child, and one who was often overprotected."

"He is, but he's a smart kid," Jack noted. "He's a smart kid who understood more than the adults around him realized. He knew his father was having an affair. Maybe he knew his father poisoned his mother, too."

"So, where does that leave you in your investigation?" Strawser was legitimately curious. "If Josh knew his father killed his mother, how does that play into a shooting in the woods?"

"We've known from the start that Josh was lying," Jack said. "Maybe he was lying because he killed his father as payback."

Strawser was taken aback. "Isn't he a little young for that?"

"It's never too late to get vengeance for your mother." Jack slowly got to his feet. "Maybe Josh was getting vengeance for more than his mother, too. Maybe he was getting vengeance for the baby as well."

"What baby?"

"The Masters had a baby who died of SIDS."

"I didn't know that. SIDS is often the diagnosis when a doctor can't come up with an underlying reason for the death of an infant. There is no test to prove it."

"What if the baby didn't die of SIDS but the mushrooms, too?" Jack asked. "I mean ... the baby died almost a year before Melanie. That would've been during morel season, too."

"A baby wouldn't be able to survive a false morel," Strawser noted. "A small piece would be enough to kill an infant."

"Yeah. That's exactly what I was thinking." Jack shook his head to dislodge the bevy of ideas floating through his brain. "I think I know someone who has a few more questions to answer. I thought she was a suspect at first, but now I'm starting to think she suspected Josh killed his father for retribution and didn't say anything. Or at least was covering up something that she didn't want to tell us about."

"Keep me informed," Strawser instructed. "I'll go through Melanie Masters' file again. I'll also pull the record on the infant and see if I can find any tissue samples on file. We might be able to run a poison panel after the fact."

"That would be great." Jack was practically vibrating with energy. "I think we're finally getting somewhere." Unfortunately for him, it was a place that Ivy would fight visiting tooth and nail.

Seventeen

"**W**here's Ivy?"

Josh was barely out of the car, ice cream cone in hand, when he began searching the nursery.

Michael, his stomach and mind troubled, flicked his young charge a frustrated look. "I already told you. She'll be here soon. She's at the hospital with Max."

"Why would she be with Max when she could be with me?"

Michael had no idea how he was supposed to answer that question. "Because Max is her brother and everyone was terrified for him yesterday." Michael managed to keep his demeanor calm, but just barely. "Ivy loves her brother. She probably arranged with her mother to pick him up."

"But ... she knew I was coming out here today," Josh persisted. "Why would she want to spend time with Max when she knew I was out here?"

"I think she believed she could do both."

"Well, that's ... not fun." Josh's face was serious as he licked his ice cream cone. "I hope she doesn't keep doing stuff like this. I won't like it if she does."

"Well, she has things to do so ... ." Michael broke off and held his hands palms up. "I guess she's going to have to do what she has to do," he said lamely.

"Yeah. Can we start in the greenhouse without her?"

"Sure." Michael shifted his eyes to the ominous sky. "It's going to storm today. I saw on the news where it's supposed to last all day. I doubt very much that we'll get very many customers. I can keep a lookout for them at the greenhouse."

Josh brightened considerably. "Then let's go. Ivy said you're the one who taught her how to do a lot of the things she does with the plants. I was hoping you could teach me."

Some of the dread and annoyance that had been wrapping around Michael's heart like a squeezing fist lessened at the boy's excited demeanor. "I think I can arrange that." He ruffled Josh's hair. "You like learning stuff, don't you?"

"Oh, I want to learn it all."

"WHERE ARE WE going?" Max asked as he picked his way through the woods, Ivy's pink hair bobbing in front of him. When his sister said she had a plan to figure things out, he had no idea it would entail hiking through the trees in search of something Ivy wouldn't identify. "How am I supposed to keep up my ruse that I need constant bed rest and nurses in skimpy outfits to take care of me if I'm seen wandering through the forest an hour after being released?"

Ivy didn't bother to hide her eye roll as she glanced over her shoulder. "You're fine."

"I had a head injury and could have died."

Ivy slowed her pace, the reality of his words setting in. "You're right. You should turn around. I'll do this alone."

Instead of making him feel better – he really was wearier than he would've been under normal circumstances – Ivy's offhand statement made Max feel like a righteous jerk. "No, no, no." He waved off the suggestion right away. "I'm going with you. I have no intention of letting something happen to you on my watch."

Ivy snorted as she turned back to her trek. "No one has to watch me. I'm perfectly capable of taking care of myself."

"I don't happen to believe that Jack feels the same way."

"And I happen to believe that Jack overreacts sometimes."

"That's what happens when you love someone." Max adopted a pragmatic tone. "Jack loves you."

"I should hope so. We're getting married." Ivy stopped long enough to close her eyes and unravel her senses. Using magic – and she could think of no other term to use even though the M-word made her leery – to help her solve something of this magnitude wasn't exactly a new thing. Her growing abilities had helped her a time or two over the past year. What was different about this particular case was the fact that she was actively trying to use her magic for a change. Before this, everything that happened had been predominantly on a passive level.

"You *are* getting married," Max agreed, watching her with unveiled interest. "I wasn't sure it would ever happen."

"Because people think I'm nutty and weird?"

"Because you close yourself off to people," Max replied without hesitation. "Because you tend to think the worst of people. I don't blame you for that. You were attacked quite often as a kid. You surrounded yourself with a protective shell. Mom, Dad, Aunt Felicity, and I helped you do it, so I know what I'm talking about."

Ivy's expression was hard to read as she focused her full attention on her brother. "Are you feeling okay? You're not lightheaded or anything, are you?"

Max made a disgusted face. "I'm being serious. It's not the head injury talking."

"Okay, but I don't exactly know what you're saying."

"I'm saying that I spent a lot of time worrying about you being happy," Max supplied. "That's all I ever wanted for you and I was afraid it would never happen. I was wrong, though. It did happen. Jack came out of nowhere and stole your heart.

"I'm not going to lie, when he first showed up I didn't want to like him on principle," he continued. "I didn't like the way he looked at you – as your older brother, that's my prerogative so don't give me grief about it – and I definitely didn't like the way he acted when he was around you. It was as if he wanted to throw himself on a live grenade at every turn, somehow protect you even though I always thought of that as my turf. I was wrong, though."

Ivy licked her lips, unsure. "Meaning?"

"Meaning that he makes you happy," Max replied. "I don't think you even realize how happy he makes you. The second he walks into a room you light up. Then, you two are like magnets gravitating toward one another. Even when I didn't like the way you looked at each other, before any of this happened, I sensed some ... inevitability, I guess that's the word ... between you guys. I knew it was going to happen."

"You didn't have faith the entire time," Ivy pointed out. "After I got shot and Jack took that brief break of his, you didn't think we would end up together then."

"That's actually not true."

Max's answer caused Ivy's eyebrows to hop toward her hairline. "You're telling me that you still believed even then? When you were ranting and raving and threatening to rip his head off, you still had faith?" Ivy was understandably dubious. "I'm calling bull on that one."

"It's true." Max refused to back down. "I was furious with him that day. I wanted to kill him. I also saw the way he was suffering. What's more important is that you saw it, too, and even though you were hurt and angry you still cared about him. That's when I knew."

"Knew what?" Ivy was honestly puzzled.

"That he was your match. I never believed in soulmates until I saw you guys together. Now, even though I understand I'm not quite ready, that's what I want in the end. I want someone who believes in me no matter what, who makes me smile even when things seem terrible, and who doesn't put up with my crap when I'm being a moron."

Ivy's shoulders stiffened. "Excuse me. I think there was an insult buried in there."

"And I think you know exactly what I'm talking about," Max countered. "You were set in your ways before Jack."

"I'm still set in my ways."

"You are, but you often take Jack's feelings into consideration and adjust what you're doing and feeling to accommodate him now, and that's something you never would've considered before," Max said.

"That's how I really knew you guys were meant to be. You put Jack first and you weren't even a little bitter about it."

"Yeah, well ... he puts me first, too."

"He absolutely does," Max agreed. "That's why I didn't kill him when I saw the way he was looking at you."

Ivy made a grumbling sound in the back of her throat. "I don't understand why we're having this conversation."

"We're having it because I want you to know how happy I am for you," Max said. "You're my baby sister and I love you. What you have with Jack is what I always wanted for you."

"I ... thank you," Ivy fumbled out. "You don't have to tell me this, though. I already know it. I've always known you want what's best for me despite the fact that you tend to let your mouth get away from you."

Max snorted, easing the serious mood. "Yes, well, I still wanted to tell you. Coming close to death makes you reevaluate things. I needed you to know how much I love you ... and how proud I am of who you've become."

"You didn't almost die," Ivy shot back, her annoyance evident. "Don't say that. You're fine."

"I am, and I intend to keep being fine. That doesn't mean I don't want to tell you how I proud I am of you."

Ivy's cheeks burned under her brother's intense scrutiny. "I love you, too."

"I know."

"You're acting like a schmuck, though."

Max broke out in a wide grin. "I know that, too. Now, come on." He prodded her forward. "Let's find whatever you think it is that Josh hid out here. I'm still not convinced you're right about this."

"I hope I'm wrong," Ivy said. "I simply don't think so."

"Well, then we'll prove you're right and move on from there. Let's get to it."

"Okay, come on." Ivy pointed toward a parcel of woods that was very familiar to her. "I think I know where we should look next."

. . .

BRIAN WAS EXPECTING Jack's call, but he was stunned by what the other detective had to say.

"You can't be serious." Brian sucked in a deep breath. "You think Josh killed his father."

"I do," Jack confirmed without hesitation. "I think that Josh somehow figured out that his father killed his mother and decided to pay him back."

"I can't see that kid as a murderer."

"I can." Jack was grim. "He has a needy way about him. He was attached to his father. Imagine finding out the man you look up to most in the world killed your mother. It had to shake him."

"But ... to plan something like this out," Brian countered. "What kind of little psychopath is capable of something like that?"

"We don't know that he planned it out," Jack said. "He could've been out in the woods with his father when he put it together, for all we know. I mean ... think about it. They're out picking mushrooms and Abraham warns Josh not to pick one of the false morels. That might have triggered a memory in Josh. He's not a little kid. He seems quite smart. If he recognized the false morel as something his father fed his mother, it could've caused him to snap."

"I guess." Brian couldn't wrap his head around it and rubbed the back of his neck. "How are you going to prove it?"

"Well, for starters, I'm heading toward Annette Hargrove's house to see if she can give me some information. After that, I'm going to see Ellen Woodbridge. I'm convinced she's hiding something."

"Fair enough. What do you want me to do?"

"Visit Tammy Vickers-Masters," Jack instructed. "She was close with the family but an outsider at the same time. Tell her what we suspect and see what she thinks. She might be able to guide us on this one."

"I can do that." Brian grabbed his keys from the corner of his desk. "Where do you want to meet up?"

"I want to play it by ear," Jack replied. "I might send you out to Ivy's nursery if we manage to confirm this, or even come close to confirming it, for that matter. Josh is out there with Michael and Ivy."

Brian realized what was worrying Jack right away. "He wouldn't hurt Ivy and Michael. You said it yourself, if he did this, he probably did it in a fugue state of sorts. He had the gun, realized what his father did to his mother, and shot him. The reason he thinks his ears didn't work is because he was in shock at what he did at the time. He can't take it back and that's why he clings to the lie. It makes him feel better."

"That's exactly what I believe."

"It's a good theory." Brian grabbed his coat and headed toward the office door. "Still, since you're hitting two of our main witnesses and I'm only hitting one, I'll head out to check on Ivy after the fact. It can't possibly hurt to keep an eye on that kid."

"Yeah. I agree."

Brian chuckled. He could practically see his partner's worried expression on the other end of the call. "Ivy can take care of herself. Don't worry about her."

"I'm not worried."

"You're always worried."

Jack turned rueful. "I can't help it. She's ... kind of my everything."

"And you're kind of schmaltzy," Brian shot back. "Don't worry about Ivy, though. I'll head out there when I'm done with Tammy."

"That sounds like a plan."

IVY SUCKED IN A BREATH and smiled when she crested the hill and found herself looking at her fairy ring. It was her favorite place in the world – other than the times she managed to climb into Jack's mind with him and have a vacation day on a sandy beach or beside a babbling brook, of course – and she'd only managed sporadic visits since the winter weather broke.

"Your fairy ring?" Max furrowed his brow as he moved to Ivy's side, confused. "You think Josh hid something in your fairy ring?"

"I think that Josh was close to this area when Abraham was attacked," Ivy replied as she moved toward the wizened tree that looked to have a craggy old face carved into it. "Think about it. Abraham was found not far that way." Ivy pointed for emphasis.

"This is the opposite direction from which Josh ran, though," Max pointed out as he matched her pace. "He would've had to run in this direction, stash the gun – yes, I know you're looking for the gun – and then run back in the opposite direction to find us."

"I don't think he knew he was going to run into us," Ivy argued. "That was a fluke. He might've known where the cottage was, though. I think his plan was to run to the cottage for help and tell his story. He ran into us first and that didn't allow him to properly prepare how he was going to explain what happened. Instead he tripped over us and had to lie on the fly."

"I still don't understand why you think Josh did this," Max pressed. "I know you said you saw him cut the tie in your vision but ... he's a kid."

"He's a disturbed kid," Ivy corrected. "He's the sort of kid who forms attachments with people and then doesn't like it when those individuals can't live up to his lofty standards. What if he decided his father couldn't give him what he needed?"

"He was the only relative Josh had left," Max supplied. "Would you kill the only lifeline you had left because he or she didn't live up to some sort of perfect ideal you'd created in your head?"

"You're assuming I would have control of that," Ivy said, her eyes moving over the fairy ring as she searched for something she was almost positive was hidden very close. "What if Josh is mentally unbalanced?"

"I guess that's a possibility." Max rubbed his chin. "Given everything that's happened to him, I can't imagine he's come out the other side unscathed. Still, to kill his father, that's cold-blooded."

"It is, but it also might have been a decision he made in the heat of the moment," Ivy said, her eyes gleaming when she caught sight of something behind the tree. "Ha!" She dived forward and rummaged behind the tree, coming out with a small camouflage bag. She didn't hesitate as she dug inside, her eyes widening as she carefully pulled out a handgun. "Do you still doubt me?"

Max was dumbfounded as he stared at the weapon. "How did you know?"

"I saw two things in my vision," Ivy replied, her breath coming out in small gasps as she stared at the gun. "The first was Josh cutting the tie on the logs. He has a small penknife, one of those things like you used to carry when you were a kid. You know what I'm talking about."

"It's called a Swiss Army Knife." Max was grim. "I can't believe the home didn't take that from him."

"He's been a real pain in the butt where the people from the home are concerned," Ivy said. "They probably didn't think they needed to search him. Or maybe he somehow came across it after the fact."

"It might have saved us some trouble if they had bothered to search him."

"I'll bring that up to Dana next time I see her," Ivy said dryly. "In fact, if you're still warm for her form, you could bring it up and force her to act as your nurse since you're still recovering."

Max's lips curved. "That right there is a genius idea."

"You can put it into motion as soon as we handle this." Ivy returned the weapon to the bag and zipped it shut. "There's no rifle out here. Josh said his father had a rifle. Why would he lie about that?"

"Maybe he thought he could get away with it."

"I guess." Ivy rolled her neck and stood. "I need to call Brian and tell him about this."

"What about Jack?"

"Jack is at the state police post in Grayling. He told me that's where he was heading. He can't help us. That means we need to call Brian."

"Well, do it." Max flicked his eyes to the trees over his shoulder. "I'm a little nervous being out in the woods now that we know what we know."

"Josh isn't out here."

"No, but he's not far away ... and he's with Dad."

Ivy's forehead wrinkled. "I forgot about that. You're right; I'll call Brian right now. Then we'll call Dad and head to the nursery. It can't hurt to keep an eye on Josh until Brian shows up."

"You read my mind."

Eighteen

Tammy Vickers-Masters didn't seem surprised to find Brian knocking on her door. She motioned him inside and offered tea, but Brian was hopeful it wouldn't be a long visit.

"I have more questions for you," he said grimly as he sat.

"I figured you probably would." Tammy leaned back in her chair and regarded him with a searching look. "Do you know who killed Abraham?"

"We have an idea who killed Abraham," Brian hedged. "What would you say if I told you that we believe Josh killed his father?"

Instead of being aghast, or reacting with surprise, Tammy merely shrugged. "I would say that was my first inclination, too."

Brian didn't bother to hide his shock. "Why didn't you say something?"

"Because you would've thought I was crazy. Oh, don't look at me that way. I always thought there was something off with that kid. Whenever I mentioned it, my husband told me I was seeing things that weren't there. No one wants to believe that there's something wrong with a child. That goes against human nature."

"You still should've told us," Brian argued. "You could've saved us some time."

"Yes, well, it didn't take you long to figure it out. May I ask what tipped you off?"

"It was several things. The first of which is that Josh's story never made sense. We initially thought he was confused because he was in shock. The more we started putting stuff together, though, the more we realized that might not be the case."

"Do you have a motive?" Tammy was the pragmatic sort who wanted all the details. "Have you figured out why he would want to kill Abraham?"

"We have." Brian bobbed his head. "We think he figured out that Abraham killed Melanie."

For the first time since he arrived, Brian arched an eyebrow as Tammy showed real surprise. "You're kidding. Are you sure that Melanie was murdered?"

"My partner just left the state pathologist's office. She told him that she was suspicious about Melanie's death from the start, but it was hard to pin down a cause. In her opinion, she's leaning toward mushroom poisoning. False morels, to be exact."

"Hmm." Tammy extended her fingers, as if stretching them to fight off a bout of arthritis. "Abraham was always a morel freak. That's not uncommon for this part of the state, though. Morels are big business. People sell them for a lot of money."

"They do," Brian agreed. "We've confirmed Abraham was having an affair. We've also received information that seems to indicate that Josh knew about the affair. He could've been holding onto a grudge for a very long time."

"Why not tell anyone?" Tammy queried. "Why wouldn't Josh simply tell the police or doctors what he suspected?"

"I have every intention of asking him that."

"What do you need from me?"

"Nothing. I simply wanted to see a reaction. Since you're not surprised, I'm pretty sure we're on the right track. In fact ... ." He broke off when his phone rang, wrinkling his nose when he recognized Ivy's number on his screen. "I apologize. Wait one second." He held up a finger and pressed the phone to his ear. "Ivy, Jack isn't with me."

Ivy wasted no time on the other end of the call. "I know. He's in Grayling. That's why I called you."

"Is something wrong?"

"Yes." Ivy sounded frazzled, causing Brian's heart rate to ratchet up a notch. "We found something hidden in the woods."

"Who is with you?"

"Max."

"Should he be out traipsing through the woods given what happened to him?"

"No, but I needed him." Ivy didn't back down. "I saw something when I visited the lumberyard. Before you ask, I'm not going to get into it. It's too much to explain and I know you don't really want to hear it."

Given some of the odd things Ivy had been doing over the past few months — sharing dreams and seeing through the eyes of a killer, for example — Brian was fairly certain that was true. "Fine. Just give me the basics."

"We found a gun," Ivy volunteered, her voice shaky. "It's a handgun and it was hidden not far from where Abraham Masters' body was found."

Brian was dumbfounded. "You're kidding me."

"I'm not. I'm heading to the nursery now. Dad is there with Josh. Can you meet us?"

"Absolutely." Brian was already on his feet. "I'm on my way."

"Thank you. I really appreciate it."

"It's my job." Something occurred to Brian. "Ivy, when you get there, be really careful. If Josh realizes that we're on to him, he might panic."

"I know. I'm worried about that, too."

"He probably won't."

"I hope so."

"Just ... be careful."

"That's the plan."

. . .

ANNETTE HARGROVE WASN'T HOME. She wasn't picking up her phone and there was no car in the driveway. Frustrated, Jack left her a message demanding she call him as soon as possible. With no other options, he headed in Ellen Woodbridge's direction. He didn't have a lot of time to waste and she was next on his interview list.

Unlike the first time he stopped by, Ellen seemed agitated when she found Jack on her doorstep for an encore interview. "Can I help you?"

"I certainly hope so." Jack was stern as he greeted her. "I don't have a lot of time to waste so I'm hopeful that you'll be able to answer some questions for me. If you could tell the truth this time, that would be great."

Ellen balked. "Excuse me? Are you accusing me of being less than truthful?" Her voice turned screechy as her eyes darted in different directions.

"Yes." Jack answered without hesitation. "Ma'am, I'm not going to pretend to understand your situation. I do know how to read people, though. I believe most of what you told us was true. However, I also believe you're leaving something out, and I'm determined to know what that something is."

To give herself time to consider the request, Ellen leaned her hip against the doorjamb and folded her arms across her chest. "I don't understand why you're even here. You can't possibly suspect me in all of this."

"To be honest, we never suspected you in the death of Abraham Masters."

Ellen looked relieved at the admission. "Well, of course not. I'm not a murderer."

"We did suspect you might have hired someone to go after him," Jack supplied. "We even thought maybe you had a boyfriend or brother in the mix. We've run a few background checks on you, though, and placed calls to your neighbors. No one has seen you with a man since breaking up with Abraham."

"You called my neighbors?" Ellen was incensed. "What gives you the right to do that?"

"I'm a police officer and I'm investigating a murder. You very clearly lied to us when we were here. We're not idiots and knew you were hiding something. That gives me the right."

Ellen worked her jaw, frustration evident.

"Ma'am, I don't have a lot of time to play games with you." Jack opted for a different tack. "I'm not trying to be difficult or ruin your life, but we have a murderer on the loose and I think you know pertinent information."

"I didn't kill Abraham." Ellen practically screamed the words. "I loved him. I thought we would end up together forever. If I killed him, that would never happen."

Jack narrowed his eyes. "You believed that even after Abraham broke up with you?"

Ellen nodded, misery clouding her round features. "I thought it was just a road bump on our way to forever." Her voice cracked as she swiped at falling tears. "You have to understand. I loved Abraham more than anything. He was my life. I truly believed we would get a chance at happily ever after."

"You said Josh walked in on you," Jack challenged. "You cleaned up that story a bit, didn't you? He didn't walk in while you were having a conversation and misconstrue something innocent, did he?"

Ellen's cheeks turned crimson. "Not exactly."

"What *exactly* happened?"

"I wasn't lying when I said that I could tell Abraham was going to break up with me," she started, uncomfortably shifting from one foot to the other. "The writing was on the wall. He was pulling away even though he knew I was going to be left with a broken heart.

"It was all Melanie's fault," she continued. "She knew about the affair and was guilting him to stay with her. That's not what he said, of course, but I knew it all the same. She was the type of woman who wanted others to be miserable just so she could be happy."

Jack didn't say it, but he was fairly convinced that Ellen was the sort of woman she just described. "If you thought Abraham was going to break up with you, why did you bother going to his house?"

"Because ... because I had to stop him."

Jack narrowed his eyes. "You mean you seduced him, don't you? You didn't give him a chance to say what was on his mind and instead you decided to get him into bed one last time. Were you going to do the old pregnancy ruse? Were you going to wait until he tried to break up with you the next time and drop the bomb that you were having a baby or something?"

"I ... no," Ellen sputtered.

Unconvinced, Jack merely shook his head. "That's exactly what you were going to do. I can't even believe it. What is wrong with you? His wife was in the hospital, dying. Did you think you would somehow get everything you wanted even though you were trying to manipulate a man who already had a family?"

"A family he didn't love," Ellen shot back. "He never loved Melanie. There was no passion there."

"And yet they had two children together."

"One child," Ellen corrected. "They had one child. That baby died. I think God realized that Melanie was using that baby as a way to keep hold of Abraham and took it away from her."

Jack felt sick to his stomach. "You're a piece of work. I think you already know that, though."

"Oh, don't look at me that way." The features Jack initially thought of as "pleasing" turned predatory. "I had every right to claim the life I wanted. If I had to do certain things to make sure that happened ... well, I'm not sorry. The only thing I'm sorry about is that someone took Abraham from me before he had a chance to realize that he made a terrible mistake when he ended things between us."

"Since that's the stuff of fairy dust and dreams, I'm going to let that go," Jack snapped. "I want to know about the day Josh returned to the house and found you with his father. You were in bed, weren't you?"

"We were." Ellen squared her shoulders, refusing to let the weight of the horrible things she'd done cause her to slouch. "We were together and basking in the afterglow. That was always our favorite time together because Abraham always gave freely of his emotions in those instances. I could tell he was thinking deep thoughts after our tryst and I was just about to ask him what he was thinking when we looked up and found Josh standing in the doorway."

Since he could picture the incident very clearly, Jack felt sick to his stomach. "And how did Josh react?"

"I don't know. It was weird."

Ellen's response caught Jack off guard. "What do you mean? Didn't he cry and throw a fit? That's how most kids would react when an affair was uncovered. I think that's pretty standard."

"He didn't freak out." Ellen was adamant. "He just stood there staring. I wasn't covered at first, but I hurried to fix that when I realized we had an audience. He didn't even look at me in that way, though."

"He was a child."

"He was a twelve-year-old boy," Ellen corrected. "Boys that age are a mess of hormones and hatred. Josh didn't react with either of those things. He just stared at us for a long time and then gave Abraham this really odd look."

"He must have said something."

"He did. He said it was time to go to the hospital. Then he turned around and walked away as if nothing out of the ordinary had happened."

Jack was legitimately flummoxed. "Why would he react like that?"

"I have no idea, but Abraham didn't seem to think it was weird," Ellen replied. "He told me to get dressed and go out the back door but that was basically it. There was no yelling or screaming. I parked at the corner of the street and watched the house. Thirty minutes later Abraham drove past with Josh in the passenger seat. Everything looked completely normal."

Jack had no idea what to make of that. "There has to be something else."

"No. That's honestly what happened. Josh didn't say a word and Abraham went chasing after him. That was basically it."

Despite himself, Jack believed her. However, he had no idea what to do with the new information.

"WE NEED TO BE CAREFUL," Max announced as he approached the nursery with Ivy, his eyes peeled as the skies overhead turned dark and threatened to open up. "It's going to storm."

"It is going to storm," Ivy agreed, her stomach churning now that she was close enough to actually confront Josh about what she knew. "I think it's going to be a big one."

As if reading her mind, Max rested his hand on Ivy's shoulder and gave it a reassuring squeeze. "It's going to be okay. It's just a storm. You love storms."

"I'm not going to love this one." Ivy was resigned as she handed Max the bag with the gun inside. "You should go into the shed and wait." She inclined her head in the direction of the building in question. "You're still weak from what happened and you don't need to be part of this."

Max wasn't happy with that suggestion one bit. "Um ... no way. I'm not leaving you alone to confront Josh. He could ... hurt you."

Ivy's expression turned rueful. "He won't, though. He hurt his father because Abraham cheated on his mother. It's entirely possible Josh believes that Abraham murdered his mother, too. We can't be sure on that front. What he did to his father was personal. He has no reason to hurt me."

"That doesn't mean he won't if he feels he's being backed into a corner."

"Yes, but I honestly don't think it will come to that." Ivy understood that was probably wishful thinking, but she didn't want Max involved in a fight given what happened the previous day. "Besides that, if Josh does go crazy, I want you in a position where you can watch without being in danger and relay any pertinent information to Brian and Jack."

Max wasn't ready to let go of his role as protective brother. "What if he attacks you?"

"He's thirteen ... and kind of small. I think I can handle him myself."

"He killed his father."

"With the gun you have possession of," Ivy reminded him. "All he has now is a Swiss Army Knife and I doubt very much he's going to try and kill me with it. There's nothing here that can hurt me."

Max wasn't convinced. "I think we should stick together."

"And I think I want you in a position to report back to Brian and Jack should it become necessary." Ivy was firm. "If he sees us together,

Josh might take it as a sign we're ganging up on him. If it's just me, he's likely to be fine."

"I guess." Max heaved out a sigh and rubbed the back of his neck. "The first sign of trouble, though, I want you to run. I want your word on it."

Ivy grinned as she pressed her hand to the spot above her heart. "I cross my heart and hope to ... ."

"Don't finish it," Max warned.

"I was going to finish it with 'make you pie.'"

"Oh." Max was properly abashed. "That sounds like a good idea. Go ahead and finish it."

Ivy giggled, some of the dread she was carrying washing away as the first raindrops fell. "Don't worry about me. Dad is here. Don't forget that. I'm sure we can handle Josh. And, if we can't, you can serve as backup."

"Okay, but if that little monster even looks at me funny, I'm giving him a wedgie."

"I would expect nothing less."

Nineteen

Ivy tried to keep her nerves at bay as she strode onto the nursery grounds, looking first to the parking lot in the hope that Brian had somehow broken every speeding law in the state in an effort to offer appropriate backup. Other than her father's car, it was empty.

Ivy sucked in a cleansing breath and went to the greenhouse first. With a storm coming, she knew Michael would herd Josh out of the elements. That was simply common sense. They were probably transplanting flowers, which was Josh's favorite thing to do, and she would be able to talk to the boy without causing a ruckus.

That was the hope anyway.

The greenhouse looked empty upon entry, which caused Ivy to slow her pace. The second greenhouse was full of seedlings, but she used this one to do the bulk of her work. The other greenhouse was nicer, the place she moved plants when they were ready to sell. This greenhouse was for work, although no one looked to be working today.

Ivy was just about ready to turn on her heel and leave, searching the other greenhouse first and foremost on her mind, but a hint of movement at the back of the building caught her eye and she stared in that direction.

Josh, an impish smile on his face, moved from behind the back bench so she had a clearer view of his diminutive figure. He had dirt on his shirt but otherwise looked happy and relaxed. His expression was enough to put Ivy at ease, at least temporarily.

"I didn't think you were in here." Ivy offered a half wave in greeting. "I was about to go looking for you. It's going to start storming any second."

"I know." Josh didn't wander far from his spot behind the bench. "I think it's going to be a big storm."

"I do, too." Even though she had no reason to be nervous, Ivy gripped her hands in front of her and glanced around. "Where is my dad? Is he out making sure everything is put away or something?"

"He's ... doing something else." Josh was blasé as he ran his fingers over the bench. "He wasn't having fun so I thought he should take a break."

There was something about the way Josh delivered the statement that set Ivy's teeth on edge. "You thought he should take a break? I'm not sure that's a good idea. He's supposed to be watching you."

"Oh, I don't need watching. I'm old enough to watch myself."

"You're very mature for your age," Ivy agreed. "You're still a child, though."

"I don't think of myself as a child."

"No?" Ivy cocked an eyebrow, her inner danger alarm starting to ping even though she couldn't identify what sort of trouble she should expect. "How do you think of yourself?"

"As an explorer." Josh stepped into the middle aisle, keeping his pace purposely slow. He didn't rush at Ivy and ask for a hug, or enthusiastically tell her what he'd been doing in the time since Michael collected him at the children's home. Instead, he merely watched in the same manner an exterminator might look at a bug before doling out the poison. "I like to experiment ... and learn things. I like to go places I've never been."

Ivy shifted her weight from left to right. Something was very wrong here. "Well, I think that's an admirable quality. Learning is one of the most important things in life. I'm still learning and I'm a lot older than you."

"My father used to say that you never stop learning."

"He was right."

"He wasn't right very often, but I think he was right about that." Josh continued his slow approach. "You're late getting here. I was expecting you an hour ago."

"I had errands to run." Ivy licked her lips as she watched the boy walk in her direction. He was the child and yet she was the one who felt unbelievably exposed. She didn't like it. "I was as quick as possible."

"What errands?"

"I had to run to the store."

Now it was Josh's turn to make a face. "Oh, now, don't lie to me. I don't like it when people lie to me."

Ivy was taken aback. "What makes you think I'm lying to you?"

"Because we saw your car at the hospital," Josh replied without hesitation. "You were with your brother."

"I picked up Max and took him home. That was one of my errands, along with running to the store."

"Uh-huh. And where is Max?"

"I just told you I took him home."

"See, I don't know if I believe that," Josh countered. "Your father said that you two are really close and that Max is always around when you need him. I think he's here with you."

"Why would I need him now?"

"Because you're acting funny."

"I was just about to say the same thing about you."

"I'm not acting funny." Josh went back to being innocent. "I'm a child. I'm acting like a child. You know ... doing things before thinking about them. That's what my mother used to say. She was always upset that I acted before I thought about the repercussions. That drove her crazy."

It was just for an instant, but somehow Ivy's mind briefly connected to Josh's and she saw a flash of a memory. He was the one projecting it – probably without realizing it – and it was at the forefront of his brain for a reason. It was from his point of view and it was enough to make her blood run cold. "I see." She inadvertently took a step back. The door was right behind her. She wasn't in immediate danger. That didn't stop the terror and disgust from bubbling up inside. "What else did your mother tell you?"

"She told me a lot of things." Josh was at the middle row of tables, taking his time as he moved forward. In her mind, Ivy pictured him approaching a stray animal with his hand extended. He wanted to lull her into a false sense of trust, but it was far too late for that. "When my sister died, she told me that accidents happen and sometimes you simply can't explain them."

"That's true." Ivy swallowed hard. "Accidents do happen. There's no rhyme or reason. Sometimes terrible things occur and there's nothing we can do to stop them."

"My mother could've stopped Jenny's death," Josh countered. "All she had to do was keep her quiet. I was nowhere near done experimenting with her, but I needed my sleep. I told my mother that and she wouldn't listen."

Ivy briefly pressed her eyes shut, the memory from Josh's head causing her stomach to flip. "You killed Jenny, didn't you?" The question was out of her mouth before she thought better about asking it. Right now, Josh was obviously playing a game. If he thought the stakes were too high, however, that game would turn into something else entirely.

Instead of denying the charge, Josh merely shrugged. "I made her stop crying. That's all she did. She cried, spit up, and crapped her diaper. I mean ... why would anyone think that's cool?"

"She was a baby." Ivy took another step back, hating that she was showing fear by retreating and yet inherently knowing it was necessary. "That's what babies do. They grow out of it, though. You did the same thing as a baby."

"Not according to my mother. I heard her talking to Aunt Annette. She said I never cried or made a fuss. She was convinced there was something different about me from the start. She didn't know I heard her say that, but people always forgot I was around ... and listening. I was always listening."

"That must have been hard for you."

"No. It helped me. I liked that they forgot about me. It made certain things easier."

Ivy had no doubt what she was dealing with now. Josh wasn't a traumatized kid with behavioral issues. He was a stone-cold killer with the face of an angel and the heart of a devil. "You poisoned Jenny."

"I learned about false morels from my father when we were hunting that year," Josh explained. He was almost to the first row of benches. After that, there was nothing standing between him and Ivy. She would have a decision to make ... and soon.

"False morels are poisonous," Ivy said automatically. "They kill people all the time."

"They do. It only took a small piece to make Jenny be quiet."

Ivy shuddered at the boy's cold tone. "And you got away with it."

"Of course I did. It was a tiny piece of mushroom. No one even suspected it was anything other than a baby going to sleep in a crib and not waking up."

"Did your parents suspect you?"

"Not at that time. I played like I was sad and they pretty much ignored me."

"That's how you liked it."

"Yup."

"What about your mother?" Things were coming together quickly in Ivy's head. She had a clear picture of Josh and how his mind worked. She wanted to kick herself for not seeing it sooner but that would have to wait for later. "You poisoned her, too, didn't you?"

"I did."

"False morels?"

"Yes, but I made a few mistakes there," Josh admitted. He was at the front of the benches but stilled his approach, giving Ivy a moment to consider what to do next as he relished telling the story of an innocent woman's horrible death. "I thought I would only need a little bit of mushroom to kill her, like Jenny."

"She was bigger, though, and stronger," Ivy surmised. "She didn't go down without a fight."

"And I couldn't keep bringing her food without looking suspicious because I rarely did that," Josh agreed. "I heard the doctors talking. She was weak and they didn't think she would survive. Then, out of nowhere, she bounced back a bit. I couldn't have that. That meant I had to do it again ... but more this time."

"But ... why? Why did you want to kill your mother?"

"Because, after Jenny died, she didn't pay any attention to me," Josh replied, unruffled. "It was supposed to be like it was before, but my mother didn't do anything but cry. She was a complete and total waste of space."

"What about your father?"

"He paid attention to me. That's why I knew it would be better when it was just the two of us."

"Things changed, though, didn't they?" Ivy prodded, shifting so she was a bit closer to the door. She had escape at her fingertips and she wasn't afraid to bolt despite the storm brewing outside. "You found out your father was having an affair with Ellen Woodbridge and that threatened your plan."

"Ellen was easy to get rid of. Dad was so worried I would tell Mom he promised to cut her loose, which he did, and then he focused on me after. That's how things were supposed to be."

"And yet you shot him in the woods," Ivy argued. "Why do that if you had everything you wanted?"

Josh shrugged, noncommittal. "It was an experiment. I wanted to see how long it would take him to die. He was starting to bother me anyway. He thought we should get counseling and stuff. Who needs that?"

Ivy rested her fingertips on the doorjamb. "I think there's more to the story. I think you didn't want to see a counselor because you knew that a professional was far more likely to see through your act. It's the same reason you didn't want to stay in the home. Those people were more likely to see the monster inside."

"I don't think monster is the right word."

"Oh, no? What's the right word?"

"I already told you that I'm an explorer."

"Yeah, well, you're a lot more than that." Ivy licked her lips and made her decision. "Where is my father? Did you do something to him?"

"Your father was a distraction," Josh replied. He seemed so calm and nice that Ivy was appropriately unnerved. "I don't like distractions."

"Is that why you cut the tie at the lumberyard? Did you think Max was a distraction, too?"

For the first time, Josh jolted at a question. He seemed surprised that Ivy had figured out that part of his evil tale. "How did you know?"

"I'm an explorer of sorts, too," Ivy replied grimly. "I just experiment in different ways."

"How?"

"It doesn't matter." Ivy put one foot on the other side of the threshold, her shoulders hopping when a terrific roar of thunder shook the building. "I think this storm is going to be a doozy."

"I think so, too." Josh almost looked pained when he snagged Ivy's gaze. "You're going to run, aren't you? You're going to abandon me. I thought you said you wouldn't do that."

"And I thought you were a kid who needed help," Ivy fired back. "You're a murderer, though. I don't want to help you any longer."

"I'm still a kid." Josh took on a pleading tone. "I don't really know what I'm doing, after all. I can't be blamed for things I don't understand."

He was worse than she ever imagined, Ivy realized. He was cold, calculating, and unbelievably smart. It was easy to see how he'd gotten away with what he was doing for so long. "I understand what you are," Ivy shot back. "And I'm not going to let you get away with it."

Ivy turned and bolted into the storm, not as much as glancing over her shoulder to see if Josh gave chase. He wouldn't have a choice in the matter. They both knew it. Josh's best chance at survival was to kill Ivy and make sure he was the only one left standing to weave a story of pain and peril. What he didn't know was that she had reinforcements. She wasn't alone in this, and that's what she held onto now as the water pelted her face and she raced through the nursery.

She had help coming. She simply needed to hold on long enough for it to get to her.

Ivy didn't waste time. She raced to the front of the nursery, to the spot where her father usually held court while regaling the guests with stories and jokes. Hopefully she would find him there, she internally rationalized, perhaps only unconscious and not terribly hurt. The small kiosk was empty.

In a moment of panic, Ivy started yelling. "Dad? Where are you? Please answer me!"

Lightning flashed in the sky in response, but she couldn't hear a voice, however weak, accompanying it. When she turned, she found Josh standing about thirty feet away. His right hand was gripped into a fist and Ivy had no doubt what he held there.

"Are you going to stab me with your knife thing, Josh?" Ivy asked as she pushed her soaking hair out of her face. "How do you think you're going to get away with it?"

"The cops never suspect me. They're not smart enough to figure it out." Josh took a step forward, his purpose evident. "You're making it harder on yourself. You should just submit."

"I think I'm good," Ivy said. "I'm not going to let you kill me. And, as for the cops, they already know you're guilty. They're on their way."

A flash of worry flitted through Josh's eyes but he quickly masked it. "I think you're making that up."

"I'm not."

"You are. If the cops knew I was the one who shot my father there's no way they would've let me hang out with you. I'm not an idiot. You guys are the idiots."

"I guess we are," Ivy agreed. "That doesn't change the fact that everyone figured things out this morning." She left out the part where they assumed Josh killed his father as retribution for what Abraham supposedly did to Melanie. That wasn't important now. "They're coming and you're going to be arrested."

"I'm a kid." Josh was back to being innocent. "You can't put a kid in prison. It doesn't happen. Even if they take me in, I'll be free in five years. I know about this stuff. I've read about it."

"That figures," Ivy muttered under her breath. "It doesn't matter. You won't get away with this."

"I already have." Josh took a menacing step forward, but he didn't make it far because a dark figure, one Ivy recognized, moved out from behind the tree to his left. It was Brian, and he didn't look happy.

"You most certainly have not." Brian grabbed Josh's wrist, the one that held the knife, and firmly squeezed. "You're done here."

Josh, perhaps realizing for the first time that he was in real trouble, widened his eyes. "You don't understand." His voice turned breathy, as if he were an innocent child who needed protection from the big, bad nursery owner. "She wanted to kill me. She was the one who killed my father. I didn't say anything before because I was afraid. It was her and Max, though. They wanted to kill him."

"And why would they want that?" Brian refused to lessen his grip on Josh's wrist even though the boy fought him tooth and nail. "How would that benefit her?"

"I don't know." Josh was solemn. "I'm innocent."

"You're pretty far from innocent, kid." Brian shoved his thumb into one of Josh's pulse points, causing him to cry out, and forced him to drop the knife. "I don't know what you are, but it's not innocent." Brian was strong so it didn't take him long to slap cuffs on Josh and then shift his attention to Ivy. "Are you okay?"

Ivy immediately started shaking her head as she moved forward. "He has my father out here somewhere. We have to find him."

Brian widened his eyes. "We'll lock him in the car and start looking. I'll call for backup."

"Hurry. I'm really worried."

"We'll find him." Brian sounded sure of himself. "Have a little faith. This bad guy is done ending lives. I promise you that."

Twenty

※

It didn't take long to find Michael. Josh hit him over the head with a shovel and dumped him in the second greenhouse, but he was alive upon discovery. Ivy and Max rode with him to the hospital, leaving Brian and the arriving cavalry to deal with Josh.

Ivy's last glimpse of the boy was through the ambulance window. He sat in the backseat of Brian's cruiser and watched the ambulance pull away. He didn't look distressed or worried, merely curious. It was that look Ivy knew would haunt her for a long time to come.

Max and Ivy were forced to sit in the lobby while Dr. Nesbitt tended to Michael. When Luna arrived, there was no force on the planet that could keep her from her husband, though, and the nurse grudgingly let her beyond the swinging double doors.

That left Ivy and Max alone, with nothing but dark thoughts to fuel them.

"I was just about to make my move when Brian showed up," Max explained, causing Ivy to shift her eyes to him. He looked bedraggled and tired but otherwise fine. "He saw me coming out of the shed and motioned me off. I wasn't sure that was the right thing to do, but I figured he knew better so I hung back."

"It turned out fine." Ivy dragged a restless hand through her snarled hair. "I just can't believe it was him all along. I mean ... I knew he killed his father. I accepted that. Mistakenly I thought he did it out of some sort of misguided loyalty to his mother."

"Yeah. It turns out he was a lot more messed up than we thought. You can't blame yourself for that."

"I think I should've seen it."

"Why? You're not omnipotent."

"I still think I should've seen something." Ivy was mired in guilt and grief. Blaming herself seemed to be a natural thing. "I can see other things. Why couldn't I see this?"

"Because you weren't looking for it," Jack answered, appearing in the doorway. He was wet, obviously had been working alongside Brian in the rain, and his expression was fierce as he strode toward her. "You can't always know everything about everyone. You're amazing, but no one is that amazing."

"Jack." Even though she'd been struggling for what felt like forever to rein in her emotions, the second she saw him, Ivy burst into tears and threw her arms around his neck. She didn't care that he was soaked to the bone. She only cared that he was with her. "I wasn't sure when I would get to see you."

"I worked as fast as I could." Jack held her close, smoothing her hair as he met Max's steady gaze over her shoulder. "Are you guys okay?"

"I wasn't even in the thick of things this time," Max replied, his heart constricting as Ivy continued to blubber against Jack's shoulder. "I knew Ivy was in trouble and was going to attack Josh from behind but that's when Brian showed up. He was quick and efficient."

"Yeah. I saw Josh in the back of the cruiser." Jack swayed back and forth in an attempt to lull Ivy. He understood this was something that would take her a bit of time to bounce back from and was in no hurry to force her to come to grips with any of it. "I talked to him."

"You did?" Ivy pulled back and swiped at the tears coursing down her cheeks. "What did he say?"

"He said a whole lot of nonsense," Jack replied. "He tried to run a story about you and Max threatening him. He said you guys killed his father and he didn't tell us that first day because he was afraid of you guys."

"Why would he say that, though?" Max challenged. "It's pretty easy to poke holes in that story."

"It is," Jack agreed, leading Ivy to a chair so he could sit and pull her on his lap. He was exhausted, working in the rain and emotional upheaval draining energy from him. He was relieved it was over, though, and knew things would be better once they could put this day in the rearview mirror. "I don't think he cares. He even owned up to stealing money from Ivy's purse so he could buy his knife, although he said it was for protection. He's used to people believing him simply because he's a kid. He's about to get a rude awakening on that front."

"What did the pathologist find?" Ivy asked, struggling to pull herself together. She didn't want anyone to see her break down, and that included Jack.

"She's still working, but I think she'll get enough that we can charge Josh with Melanie's murder. Jenny's might be more difficult, but we'll see. Brian said Josh admitted all of it to you, so you'll probably have to testify."

"Gladly."

Jack knew that was the last thing she wanted to do, no matter what she said, but he didn't push her on the matter. "I talked to Ellen Woodbridge. She admitted Josh saw her having sex with Abraham. I thought that propelled our first theory – that Josh was out for revenge against his father – until she described the way Josh reacted. Right then I knew something was wrong, that we were missing something."

"I didn't realize until he started acting weird in the greenhouse," Ivy admitted, running her fingers over the hand Jack held at her waist. "I still thought we were dealing with a misguided kid until he opened his mouth."

"You must have been afraid." Jack kissed her temple. "I'm sorry. I was too far away to get to you. I felt a bit of your fear when I was driving. It killed me knowing that I wouldn't get to you in time."

"You can't always be the hero." Ivy offered up a rueful smile. "Even if Brian didn't arrive in time, I would've figured out a way to take him down."

"I know you would have. You're my strong girl." Jack snuggled her in close. "Still, that was a lot for you to deal with. Brian said you found the gun."

Ivy bobbed her head. "I did. He hid it behind the tree in my fairy ring. His father was killed fairly close to that location. He didn't go far to hide the gun. He must have realized he only had a limited timetable to work with."

"How did you even know to look there?" Max asked. "You didn't tell me."

"I told you about the flash I had at the lumberyard, though," Ivy reminded him, digging in her pocket for the ties. "By the way, you'll need these for your case." She dropped them in Jack's hand. "Josh cut one of them because he wanted to hurt Max. That was his intent from the start the day Max took him for the afternoon. He said Max was a distraction."

"I think Josh didn't like distractions because he desperately needed to be the center of attention," Jack offered. "He's a messed-up kid."

"I think he's a sociopath," Ivy countered. "I don't think he has any emotions, although he's good at mimicking them. That's what I saw in my vision, although I didn't understand it at the time. In addition to seeing him cutting the ropes at the lumberyard, I also saw a face I recognized. It was the face on the tree. That's how I knew where to look for the gun."

"Well, you did a good job." Jack gave her another kiss. "I kind of wish you hadn't approached him yourself, but I understand why you did it. You were still toiling under the assumption that what happened to Abraham Masters was some sort of tragic accident or revenge scheme, something that Josh could explain away."

"I didn't think he could explain away his father's death," Ivy clarified. "I just thought that with counseling ... I don't know ... I thought maybe he could get better."

"I don't think getting better is in the cards for Josh." Jack stretched out his long legs and kept Ivy flush against his chest as he reclined in the chair. "How is your father?"

"He's awake," Max replied. "We found him in the second greenhouse. He was hazy but said Josh smacked him over the head. He thinks it was with a shovel. I have a feeling Josh was probably going to go back and finish him off later, but he was more interested in getting to Ivy."

"Yeah, he seemed to hone in on her from the start," Jack agreed.

"I think it was because he thought he could manipulate me," Ivy admitted. "He thought I was an easy mark."

"I don't think that," Jack countered. "I think he looked at you and saw something interesting. By his own admission, the kid liked to learn. He thought you could teach him stuff. He thought you had time and attention to give. That's all he really cared about."

Ivy rested her head on Jack's shoulder, allowing herself to breathe and absorb some of his warmth. "What will happen to him now?"

"He'll be locked up in a state facility and observed for a bit," Jack answered, moving his hand to the back of Ivy's neck so he could rub away some of the tension accumulating there. "There are going to be a lot of doctors and therapists studying him for the foreseeable future."

"He might like that," Ivy noted. "He likes learning things. Maybe they can teach him something about his own nature."

"That is a frightening thought."

The trio lapsed into amiable silence, allowing it to stretch until Luna returned to the lobby. She looked relieved, a warm smile on her face as she regarded them. "He's going to be fine."

"That's good." Ivy blew out a sigh as she straightened. "Is he angry? It's my fault he got dragged into this."

"He's not angry." Luna's smile never wavered. "He does insist that you make him morel soup, morel salad, and morel pasta with Alfredo sauce during his convalescence, though. It seems Max comes by his need to be babied while injured naturally."

Ivy laughed. It felt good to let some of the pain wash away. "I'll get on that tonight. Are they keeping him here for observation?"

"They are. After that, he'll be home."

"I'll have the soup and salad ready for tomorrow. The pasta the next day."

"That sounds good." Luna moved closer to her daughter, perhaps sensing that Ivy was at her limit and needed something to pick up her spirits. "Your father said to tell you that he wasn't worried even after he was knocked out. He knew you would come to his rescue."

"How did he know that?" Ivy was honestly curious. "When I couldn't find him, I was so afraid that it was already too late. How could he possibly know I would come through?"

"Because you're you." Luna tweaked her nose. "Like it or not, Ivy Morgan, you're strong and people have faith in you. There's no reason to blame yourself for what happened here. You couldn't have possibly known what that child was."

Ivy wanted to believe her. "I think it's going to take me a little bit of time to let it go."

"Oh, I know." Luna's eyes twinkled. "That's what you have Jack for, though. He'll help you through this."

"Yes, I'm sure he will," Max drawled. "It will involve kisses ... and heavy petting ... and me wanting to blacken his eye for being a pervert."

Rather than being offended by Max's words, Jack merely smiled. "It sounds like we're going to have a nice couple of days, huh? Relaxing."

Max scowled. "That's not what I said."

"And yet it's what I heard." Jack smacked a kiss against Ivy's cheek. "Come on, honey. Let's see your dad and then I'll take you home. I think we both need a quiet night together."

The notion was enough to elicit a genuine smile from Ivy. "I think that's definitely the best offer I've had all day."

Jack offered her a flirty wink. "I aim to please."

"And you rarely miss."

"Ugh," Max groaned. "Can I be unconscious again, too? I don't want to hear this."

"Live with it." Jack drew Ivy to her feet. "It's not going to change. You're stuck with me for the long haul."

Max made a face. "I guess I can live with that."

"We can all live with that." Luna beamed. "We're one big, happy family. Who doesn't want to live with that?"

It was a simple question that didn't need an answer, but Ivy had one all the same. Josh didn't want to live with that.

Yes, the boy with the angelic face and the cold heart was definitely going to haunt her. She would have to find a way through it. Thankfully, she wouldn't be alone.

Made in the USA
Las Vegas, NV
12 January 2023